THE DISAPPEARANCE

READ ALL THE MYSTERIES IN THE
HARDY BOYS ADVENTURES:

COMING SOON:

HARDY BOYS
ADVENTURES

#18 *THE DISAPPEARANCE*

FRANKLIN W. DIXON

ALADDIN   New York London Toronto Sydney New Delhi

ALADDIN

An imprint of Simon & Schuster Children's Publishing Division

1230 Avenue of the Americas, New York, NY 10020

First Aladdin paperback edition February 2019

Text copyright © 2019 by Simon & Schuster, Inc.

Cover illustration copyright © 2019 by Kevin Keele

THE HARDY BOYS MYSTERY SERIES, HARDY BOYS ADVENTURES, and related logos are trademarks of Simon & Schuster, Inc.

Also available in an Aladdin hardcover edition.

All rights reserved, including the right of reproduction in whole or in part in any form.

ALADDIN and related logo are registered trademarks of Simon & Schuster, Inc.

For information about special discounts for bulk purchases, please contact Simon & Schuster Special Sales at 1-866-506-1949 or business@simonandschuster.com.

The Simon & Schuster Speakers Bureau can bring authors to your live event. For more information or to book an event contact the Simon & Schuster Speakers Bureau at 1-866-248-3049 or visit our website at www.simonspeakers.com.

Series designed by Karin Paprocki

Interior designed by Mike Rosamilia

The text of this book was set in Adobe Carlson Pro.

Manufactured in the United States of America 0119 OFF

2 4 6 8 10 9 7 5 3 1

Library of Congress Cataloging-in-Publication Data

Names: Dixon, Franklin W., author. | Title: The disappearance / by Franklin W. Dixon. Description: First Aladdin hardcover/paperback edition. | New York : Aladdin, 2019. | Series: Hardy boys adventures ; #18 | Summary: While at a comic book convention, the Hardy brothers and Frank's new girlfriend Jones meet up with Jones's online friend Harper, but when she disappears overnight, the brothers start looking into her life and uncovering her secrets.

Identifiers: LCCN 2018037375 (print) | LCCN 2018043895 (eBook) | ISBN 9781534414907 (eBook) | ISBN 9781534414884 (pbk) | ISBN 9781534414891 (hc) Subjects: | CYAC: Missing persons—Fiction. | Brothers—Fiction. | Mystery and detective stories. | BISAC: JUVENILE FICTION / Mysteries & Detective Stories. | JUVENILE FICTION / Action & Adventure / General.

Classification: LCC PZ7.D644 (eBook) | LCC PZ7.D644 Df 2019 (print) | DDC [Fic]—dc23

LC record available at https://lccn.loc.gov/2018037375

CONTENTS

GEEKING OUT 1

JOE

"**Y**OU GUYS," MY BROTHER'S GIRLFRIEND, Jones, suddenly gasped, staring at her phone with her mouth hanging wide open. "*Oh. My. Gosh.* Did you know—"

"That the whole cast of *Mercury Man* will be there, signing autographs?" Frank finished, then pulled off the Garden State Parkway, following the exit for Atlantic City. "Yeah, but unfortunately, it's a ticketed event. We would have had to get our tickets, like, six months ago. And we didn't even know each other then!"

Jones beamed at him from the passenger seat ("Girlfriends automatically get shotgun," Frank had told me with some regret as he'd kicked me out of the seat when we picked up Jones) but shook her head, her straight black hair, cut just below her chin, barely moving. "I can't believe we've only known each other for a month. Like, was there ever a time we weren't together? But no . . . I was going to tell you that Breakwater Comics is going to have a booth." She pressed a button to put her phone to sleep and placed it in her lap. "*Tiny* little comics store in Portsmouth, New Hampshire, but they have this amazing website. The owner is almost more like a curator than a straight seller—he finds some *amazing* stuff." She let out a satisfied sigh, settling back in the seat and looking straight ahead. "I'm going to check out his booth, like, first thing."

"*After* we go by the Hellion booth to get our free comic," Frank said with a smile. "Remember? They're only printing it for this convention."

"Oh my gosh," Jones replied. "I can't believe I almost forgot. There's just so much to get excited about!"

In the backseat, I cleared my throat. "Like lunch!" I put in. "Remember, you guys said we could check out the boardwalk. I want to get some saltwater taffy."

That might sound a little childish. But saltwater taffy, especially consumed on a boardwalk, just minutes after it was pulled, is freakin' amazing. That's a fact.

Jones turned back to me with a slightly surprised look, like she'd forgotten I was there. "Oh, of course, Joe," she said. "The Comic-Con is in Boardwalk Hall, which is right there. But maybe after we do all the time-sensitive things at the convention."

What am I doing? I wondered. I waited until she turned around before frowning out at the flat sandy land that bordered the Atlantic City Expressway. How had I, Joe Hardy, Relatively Cool Guy, ended up spending the first Saturday of my spring break driving to a *comic book convention* in Atlantic City with my older brother and his girlfriend? Surely there were cooler things I could be doing, like—well, anything.

It's not that I don't like comics, or, more specifically, comic book movies. I went to see *Wonder Woman* and *Black Panther* like everyone else, and I will admit, they were totally awesome. But unlike Frank, I don't have whole boxes of comic books hidden under my bed, and I can't spend hours debating with you which Doctor Who was the best or whether the campy *Batman* television series from the 1960s should be considered "canon" or not.

Know who can, though? *Jones.*

Jones isn't bad. I mean, she's pretty cool. She's really friendly and never seems to have a problem with my hanging out with them, even if I sigh loudly and roll my eyes every time they start to act mushy. She's also supersmart. She's probably smarter than Frank. Jones is homeschooled, which means she helps set her own curriculum and decides what she wants to study. So she has a wealth of knowledge about random, obscure topics, and she can spend hours telling you interesting facts about octopi (that's more than one octopus, FYI) or the history of Barbados or who assassinated James Garfield (it was this weird guy named Charles Guiteau—look him up).

Yeah, Jones is pretty cool. The thing is—ever since Frank met her at a book signing last month, he and Jones have been *inseparable*. I wake up on a Saturday morning, and whereas Frank and I used to laze around on the couch watching Netflix until noon, now *Jones* is there, and she's brought over some obscure DVD of a Danish movie about a shark person. And she and Frank are, like, making clever little quips to each other about this extremely depressing Danish movie about a *shark person*, and I'm like, "Hey, wanna watch *Stranger Things* again?" and Frank is like, "Maybe some other time, Joe," and then Jones offers me popcorn and I just want to punch something. Or also, like, yell, *Don't you have a home?!* which I know is unfair and not the nicest way to treat a cool person like Jones.

See, it's not usually like this. Usually *I'm* the person bringing girls around, or bagging on plans with Frank to hang out with a girl I like. Which maybe means I should be more understanding, but also means that I'm just not *used to* having to share Frank with a girl. And—honestly—I kind of miss the guy. Usually, it's the Frank and Joe show, all the time, everywhere, with the two of us teaming up to solve mysteries and eat lunch together and make clever in-jokes about *Stranger Things* on a Saturday morning. So it's not *bad* that Frank has found someone he really likes in Jones—I get that.

It's just . . . different.

But it's cool. I'll get used to it. I *want to* get used to it.

Which was why, when Frank came home a couple of

weeks ago all jazzed that Jones had told him about this Comic-Con (not the *huge* Comic-Con, but a small, local one) that was happening in Atlantic City, which was within driving distance from our house, I asked if I could tag along.

Frank, bless him, was like, "Yeah, Joe, that would be awesome!" He seemed genuinely excited, maybe because I have a tendency to fall asleep when he tries to tell me cool stories from his comic books.

And I will admit—I was *kind of* supposed to be studying for the SAT, which I was going to take for the second time a week from today. According to my parents, this spring break would be an "excellent opportunity to really drill down and study hard." To drive this point home, my mom went to the library and borrowed approximately 3,684 SAT prep books for me to study. Who even knew you could take out that many books?

Anyway, I don't *love* studying. Who does, when it's a beautiful spring day and the sun is shining?

So here I was. In a car. Headed to Comic-Con with my brother and his girlfriend.

Who were making moony eyes at each other.

"Frank, watch the road!" I yelled.

Frank turned back to the highway just in time to notice a Volkswagen swinging into the lane ahead of him. "Whoa! Where'd *he* come from? Anyway, Jones, did Harper text you?"

"Who's Harper?" I asked Jones. "Friend of yours from the Last Names as First Names Club?"

She snorted and shook her head. "Very funny, Joe. No, she's a girl I know from the InkWorld online community." She lifted up her phone again and began scrolling through it. "Oh, yeah. She texted about half an hour ago, I forgot I had my phone on silent. She says she can meet us on the boardwalk when we get there—near Sandee's Frozen Banana Shack. It's right across from the hall where the convention is."

I pulled out my phone and Google Mapped it. "Ooh, it's also right across from the Fiorelli Saltwater Taffy shop," I said.

"Perfect!" cried Jones, turning around to me with a bright white smile.

"See," Frank said, pulling off the Atlantic City Expressway, "I can just tell this is going to be an amazing day. There's something for everybody!"

"Oh. My. Gosh! I can't *believe* it!"

Jones, Frank, and I were wandering through the con-related crowd, around the off-season snack shops and souvenir stands—some open, others closed—when Jones suddenly cried out and took off.

I couldn't say anything, because my mouth was filled with saltwater taffy. Peanut butter, by the way, is by far the best flavor. But Frank looked at me and nodded in the direction Jones disappeared in, like, *Shall we follow her?* I nodded back, like *sure.*

We passed through a big group of middle school girls,

who were all comparing their superhero costumes—most popular component: tinfoil—and emerged to find Jones hugging an older girl. The girl was in her midtwenties, maybe, with a big smile and long, wavy auburn hair tied back with a black-and-white scarf. She was wearing a T-shirt that said *I AM WONDER WOMAN, THANKS FOR NOTICING*.

She was cute, I couldn't help but observe.

Jones let the girl go, and the girl—Harper, I was guessing—looked around the boardwalk with a furrowed brow like she was searching for someone. Then she quickly turned back to Jones, all smiles.

Hmm, I thought. *Wonder who else she could be looking for?*

"It's *so* amazing to meet you in person," she told Jones. "I feel like I know you already! You always make the best comments, and we've had all these long private conversations."

Jones grinned. "You're like my online sister," she said. "Which is *way* better than a real-life sister, because I don't have to share a bedroom."

Harper laughed, shaking her head. "That's so funny," she said, "because my boyfriend, Matt, always jokes about how he's sharing me with you and all my online buddies."

Boyfriend. Well, there it was. Even if I could somehow convince Harper to fall for a teenager, she was taken.

Bummer.

After introducing Frank and me to Harper, Jones gestured to the entrance to the convention hall, teeming with other comic fans, some in costume, some not. "Shall we go?"

she asked. "The earlier we get in, the more free stuff there'll be for the taking!"

Harper nodded. "Let's go," she said.

Frank grabbed Jones's hand and squeezed it, beaming like Stan Lee himself just called up and asked him out to dinner. "I can't wait," he said. "You guys, this is the *best* day."

And just like that, a little of my crankiness evaporated.

Even a cool guy like me couldn't argue with something that made my bro this happy.

The convention was more fun than I thought it would be. Especially since I didn't know anyone there and could geek out with my geeking-out crew.

We walked through a whole interactive exhibit one company had put up to promote their new movie, *Mercury Man*, and even though we hadn't gotten tickets to the panel discussion, Frank managed to snap up a signed copy of the poster at one dealer's booth. "I'm going to hang it over my bed," he announced, his big smile making him look a lot like his twelve-year-old self.

Then we checked out the sellers' floor, which was huge enough to spend a week in. We strolled lazily along the aisles, splitting up to check out things that interested us and then catching up with one another. Harper was way into indie comics, so she disappeared for a while into this booth that was filled with indies from all over the country. And Jones was a huge TornadoGirl fan, so she spent a long time talking to a woman who had a booth dedicated to that character. This woman even made her own collages inspired by the series, which Jones thought were really cool.

And me? Well, I found a lot more exciting stuff than I expected to. I got lost for a while in this graphic novel booth, poring over books based on characters I'd never heard of before. It was crazy how deep they got, how dark some of them were. I ended up buying three to check out later.

"Having fun?" Harper asked me with a grin when I caught up to her outside the graphic novel booth.

"I am," I admitted. "Kind of more than I expected to."

She nodded. "Yeah, I remember my first convention. I thought I'd find maybe a couple things I was into, but the whole thing was just amazing. It was like this portal into a world I'd never known existed, but where I wanted to disappear."

I wouldn't go that far, I almost said, but clutching my bag of graphic novels, I had to admit I didn't know. Maybe I *would* get way into the comics-geek lifestyle. Maybe next year, it'd be me in a tinfoil costume!

But probably not.

As we walked down the aisle to catch up with Jones and Frank, who were talking to what looked like a droid, Harper glanced to the side and suddenly flinched. She stopped and turned back, staring at whatever had spooked her and looking for a second like she was going to duck down another aisle. But then her expression smoothed out, and she stood up to her full height again, striding casually back over to me like nothing happened.

"Um, you okay?" I asked, looking pointedly from her to the direction where whatever spooked her was.

She shook her head and let out a little chuckle, which sounded (to my trained detective ear) a little fake. "Oh, I'm fine," she said. "It's going to sound stupid. I'm crazy afraid of mice, and I thought I saw something scurrying along the floor."

Except you were looking at something person-height off the ground, I thought, *not at the floor.*

I almost said something, but then I wondered if I was the one being weird. Solving mysteries all the time can make you turn everything into a mystery. Maybe Harper was scared of something, or someone. Or maybe she just thought she saw an ex-boyfriend and didn't want to talk about it. Really, that was the more likely option.

"There's Frank and Jones," I said, nodding at a booth just ahead of us. "Should we catch up?"

"Sure," said Harper, and began hurrying toward them. I sped up too, but then Harper paused to look at some vintage Batman stuff the vendor next to the droid-guy was selling. I kept going, because Frank had turned around and was waving me over.

"Can you *believe* this?" he asked, gesturing to the shiny silver robot, which looked like it was watching Frank with a polite expression.

"Is this your friend?" the robot asked in an electronic voice. There was a musical beeping sound. "Based on the similarities in your facial features, I predict that he is your brother."

Frank laughed. "Oh my gosh, yes!" He looked at Jones, who was standing just on the other side of the robot, watching the whole scene, giggling with delight. "This is Joe."

"Joe . . . *Hardy*," the robot said, turning its flashlight eyes on me. They dimmed, then slowly lit back up, like it was taking me in. "Approximately . . . sixteen years old?"

Now I was weirded out. "Frank, did you tell it that?"

Frank shook his head. "No. Well, I told him our names. But he figures everything else out himself, because he's been programmed with top-of-the-line facial recognition software."

I glanced at the robot, which was still facing me, its eyes fully lit now. Then I moved away, frowning at Frank. "It kinda creeps me out."

Frank laughed. "Why?" he asked. "He's just a harmless robot."

"How do you know that?" I asked. "Maybe its job is to collect data and sell it to marketing companies or something."

Jones raised her eyebrows. "That's a very valid concern, Joe, but I don't think we have anything to fear from FriendBot here. Sometimes people just use technology for fun!" Then she frowned, looking behind me. "Where's Harper?"

"She was—" I moved even farther from the robot, gesturing to the booth where Harper had paused to look at the Batman stuff. "Huh. That's weird. She stopped right there. . . ." I scanned the other booths nearby but still couldn't find her. In fact, now I didn't see her on the aisle at all.

Frank said good-bye to FriendBot, and then we all moved away from the booth into the aisle. "Maybe she had to use the restroom or something?"

"I guess . . . ," Jones began, but she was cut off by a young-ish guy with a blue-dyed buzz cut wearing a military jacket, who suddenly materialized in front of us.

"Excuse me," he said, "but did I see you earlier with a girl about so high"—he indicated about five foot nine—"with long reddish hair and pink lipstick?"

Frank expression's turned suspicious, but if Jones had any concerns about this guy, she didn't show it. "Yeah, I think that's my friend Harper," she said. "Have you seen her? We seem to have lost her."

The guy smiled, shaking his head. "I was going to ask you the same thing. See, I was hoping to introduce myself. Well, we've been talking online for a long time but I've never met her in person. We both post on this online comics forum called—"

"*InkWorld?*" Jones asked, excitedly reaching out to touch the guy's arm. "Omigosh, who are you? My username is JonestheAvenger!"

"Oh, wow!" The guy's eyes lit with recognition. "We

comment on each other's posts all the time! I'm ComiczVon. I mean, Von. Von is my real-life name."

Jones laughed. "And my real-life name is Jones. This is my boyfriend, Frank, and his brother, Joe."

Von looked at each of us, nodding.

Jones sighed. "I wish I could introduce you to Harper," she said, "but we seem to have lost her."

"Yeah, what a bummer," Von agreed, looking down at his shoes. "I really . . . I would have liked to meet her. Anyway, can I give you my card to give to her? I'm a comic-book dealer, and I live right nearby. Maybe we could meet up before she leaves."

"That would be fun," Jones said enthusiastically, taking the guy's card. "Have you had a good convention?"

"Really good," Von said. "Yeah, it was great to meet you. I have to run now, I have to meet up with a vendor, but maybe I'll see you again?" He gestured to the card.

"Sounds good," Jones replied. "Enjoy the rest of the con!"

The guy darted off down the aisle, and Frank, Jones, and I all looked at one another, like *What do we do now?*

"I guess we could just keep looking at booths for a while," Frank suggested. "Harper might turn up again. And if not, at least we'll get to see more."

Jones and I agreed, and the three of us continued our slow-and-casual walk up and down the aisles, pausing to look at things, separating and meeting up again. But something was nagging at me, keeping me from getting really interested in anything I saw. *What happened to Harper?* I couldn't help but think of the fear on her face when she saw whatever it was she saw earlier, the thing she claimed was a mouse.

After another half hour or so, there was an announcement over the loudspeaker. The convention was closing in fifteen minutes. It would open again tomorrow at ten, but we'd only bought tickets for today.

Frank groaned, but Jones shrugged. "We should probably be heading back anyway," she said, but her eyes were darting all over the convention floor—still looking for Harper, I figured. "We've seen about everything there was to see. This was fun!"

But her voice was missing some of the enthusiasm she'd had that morning. I had the feeling we were all wondering what happened to Harper. Even if she'd just wandered off and gotten involved in something else—wasn't she even going to say good-bye?

We slowly made our way to the exit, pausing to use the restrooms and watch the trailer for a new science fiction series debuting next fall. We walked out the door onto the nearly dark boardwalk, which was gusty and cold, despite it *supposedly* being spring. March in the Northeast is the worst.

"Does anybody remember where—?" Frank began, but before he could finish, a purple-coated auburn-haired figure dove out from behind a lemonade stand and tackled us.

"You guys!" Harper cried. "I am so, so sorry I lost you. I

had to take a call from my boyfriend, Matt—he's a worrier. So I went outside for some privacy, but when I came back, you guys were gone. I couldn't find you."

That seemed a little weird, because the three of us had stayed in the same aisle for a while, waiting for her. I suddenly remembered the way Harper had looked around the boardwalk when we'd first met her—skittish, almost, like she was afraid someone might see her. I thought of Von, and the card he'd given Jones. Had Harper ducked out to avoid him, maybe?

Was someone after her?

But before I could think on that too much, Jones pulled the card out of her pocket and pushed it at Harper. "Omigod, you will not believe who I just met—ComiczVon from InkWorld! He was totally nice, and he just missed you—he really wanted to say hi. So he gave me this card."

Harper reached out and took it, looking down at the information with a thoughtful expression that I couldn't quite read. Was it scared? Or just curious?

"Maybe we could meet up with him for dinner!" Jones went on, clearly excited. "I'm starving, actually. I heard there's a good Mexican place one town over. We could give Von a call, tell him to meet us there?"

Now Harper's face changed. For just a second, she seemed to pale. But at just that moment, the lights on the boardwalk came on, casting blue light on everything. Had she really turned pale, or was it just the changing light?

"You know," she said, her expression turning back to its usual friendly self, "I'm actually kind of beat. Is that awful, to be this antisocial? But I *would* like to keep hanging out with you guys—and maybe get something to eat." She slipped the card into her pocket. "I can send Von a note tomorrow. Maybe we could meet up before I leave."

Jones nodded. "Sure, no problem! We could all get Mexican, just the four of us?"

"I have an even better idea." Harper's eyes sparkled in the bluish light. "I rented a place for the night—just a UrMotel apartment a couple towns over. It's actually pretty great, it's on the beach, and it has a TV and stuff." She smiled. "What if we just go there and order a pizza? We can relax, hang out, and chill for a while."

"That sounds great," I said, maybe a little too quickly. But honestly, she had me at "pizza." My stomach let out an enthusiastic growl.

Jones chuckled. "Well, Joe is in," she said, smiling at Frank. "What do you think?"

"Sounds good to me," he said. "We'll need to get on the road in a couple hours, but it sounds like the perfect end to a perfect day."

And surprisingly, I totally agreed with my brother.

PARTY POOPER 2

FRANK

I WAS ALREADY IN A PRETTY GREAT MOOD WHEN WE pulled up to the apartment complex where Harper was staying. I mean, how many days like this does a guy get? Hanging out, meeting super-fun comics people, getting to look at and learn about something you love—all with the coolest girl you've ever met! Oh, and Joe.

Joe seemed to be having a lot better time than I'd expected. "This is the place? It looks awesome," he said as I parked and we all climbed out of the car. He wasn't wrong. The complex was high-end-looking, with bright white walls and an outdoor system of stairs and walkways with railings. Behind the complex, sand stretched out toward darkness in the distance, and we could hear waves lapping the shore.

Pretty swanky digs for someone not much older than us.

Harper was pulling her little blue sports car into a space across from us. After a few seconds, she emerged, smiling.

"This place really is right on the beach!" Joe said. "I mean, I know you said that, but there's right on the beach and there's *right on the beach*, you know?"

Harper laughed. "I know," she said. "The apartment is pretty nice too. I checked in this morning."

"You were able to check in this morning?" Jones asked, looking puzzled. "Don't most hotels make you wait till the afternoon?"

"This isn't a hotel, it's a UrMotel," Harper explained. She began leading us toward the complex lobby. "It's a website that helps connect people who want to rent out their places with people who want to rent them. I like to use it because it ends up being cheaper than a real hotel—plus, it's a little homier. Like here, I have a whole apartment—not just a bed and a desk, you know?"

Joe nodded. "Yeah, I've heard of them," he said. "But does that mean you're staying with someone?"

Harper shook her head. "Not in this case. Every host handles things a little differently, but this host sent me the security codes for the front door and the apartment door, so I haven't even met her. I have her number if I need anything, though. She lives nearby. She owns a few of these units, and she rents them out."

We'd reached the front gate. Harper pulled out her phone and clicked around for a bit, then read the code and punched it into the security pad. With a click, the front gate opened. We all walked in and entered a bright white lobby decorated with color-saturated photos of the beach. There was a sand-colored leather couch and two chairs in a corner, and mailboxes lined one wall. It all looked pretty nice.

We followed Harper through the lobby and out the back door. It led to a small patio facing the beach, with stairs leading up to walkways on different levels. Harper swung a left and headed up the stairs. "Don't worry," she called behind her, "I'm only on the second floor."

As we climbed, a family of four—mom, dad, a boy of about five, and a toddler girl—came down the stairs. The mom nodded at Harper and smiled. "Did you have fun at Comic-Con?"

Harper smiled back. "Sure did," she said. "Even found some friends there!"

"That's great," the mom said, trailing her family down to the patio. "Have a good night!"

After we'd all reached the second-floor walkway, Harper turned to face us. "They're UrMotel guests too," she said. "Same host. I met them this morning."

"This seems like a really cool place," Jones said. "I just hope it has good pizza."

Harper laughed. "Well, there are a bunch of take-out menus in the room. We can see which one sounds the best."

She led us down the walkway, past a few locked doors, to apartment 2F.

Many of the apartment doors had tiny keypads, just

like the front door. I guessed these were the ones that were rented out to tourists, through UrMotel or other sites. Harper clicked around on her phone again, then tapped the code onto the pad. With a softer *click*, the door unlocked and swung open.

"Here we are," said Harper, walking in and switching on the light. She turned to us and swept her arm across the room. "Home sweet home!"

Inside, the apartment was also painted bright white. It was clean and modern, with brightly colored furnishings. A huge flat-screen TV was mounted to the right wall, and a squishy-looking red couch faced it, holding an array of cozy-looking pillows and a fluffy blanket. A small galley kitchen led off the back wall.

Two doors stood to the left of the television. "Oh, you guys can look around," Harper offered. "I don't mind at all. I'm still learning my way around the place." She opened both doors and turned on the lights. The room on the left was a modern bathroom, filled with clean, folded towels; on the right was a small but tidy bedroom. It had a full-size bed covered with an orange duvet.

"This is really sweet," Jones said, poking her head into each room. "Is it rude of me to ask—was it expensive?"

"Not at all." Harper shook her head. "It's not really beach season yet, so I got this place for about what I would have paid for a decent motel in the suburbs," she explained. "But it's *so* much comfier."

"Agreed," said Joe with a nod. "This place is really great. But, guys, can we talk about what's really important?"

Harper and Jones both looked surprised. "What's that?" Jones asked.

Joe pointed to a file folder on the kitchen counter, bursting with take-out menus. "Which of those places can get me a pizza the fastest? I'm *starving*!"

An hour and a half later, satiated, we were all lying around on the couch and on some pillows Jones and Harper had moved to the floor. An empty pizza box was on the coffee table in front of us, and we'd moved on to a pretty intense conversation.

"Seriously, though," Jones was saying, gesturing with a pointed finger, "Batman has *no superpowers*. He wasn't, like, bitten by a radioactive spider, or born on another planet. And yet he's still out there, kicking butts, doing his best to keep Gotham safe."

"But Gotham is still kind of crummy, right?" Joe asked. "I mean . . . *I* would never choose to vacation there. Like, from what I see in the movies."

Jones rolled her eyes. "He's doing his best, okay, dude? It's not like he's getting a lot of help from those corrupt cops."

"I just like Superman better," Joe said with a shrug.

"Oh my God," moaned Jones, burying her face in the huge pillow she was leaning on.

"Do you even *like* comics?" Harper asked him with a giggle. "No offense, you just seem a little . . . new."

Joe turned to face her, his expression the picture of sincerity. "I like comics very much," he said.

I tried to stifle my laugh. "Joe saw *Black Panther* twice," I said, trying to be a supportive brother. *Because he liked the rhino wearing armor,* I added silently.

But Joe was busy digging his own hole. "I think comics are very," he was saying, "very . . . *colorful*."

Jones let out a loud bark of a laugh, and Harper dissolved into giggles.

"What?" asked Joe.

"They're also rectangular," I said drily. "And have lots of lines and bubbles."

Jones and Harper laughed harder, and even Joe looked a little sheepish and shook his head, chuckling.

"Maybe I am kind of a newbie," he admitted.

"It's cool, Joe," Harper said, getting up to walk to the counter and grab another soda. "You had fun today, right? So maybe you're a—"

Bang! Bang! Bang!

Three loud bangs on the door cut Harper off, and we all looked toward it in surprise.

"What on earth . . . ?" Harper muttered.

"Do you know anyone here?" Jones asked, standing up and looking a little concerned. "Like, besides us and ComiczVon?"

"Or the family we met on the way up," I added.

But Harper was shaking her head, walking slowly toward the door. "No one in that family would bang on my door that hard."

"*Open up!*" a man's voice yelled from the walkway. "I know you're in there! I've been listening to your partying all night!"

"Partying?" Joe asked, frowning and standing up.

I was confused too. We'd been goofing around and eating pizza. We were having fun, but it was hardly a party.

Looking irritated, Harper went to the door and swung it open. "Listen," she said, "I think—"

But the man who was standing there, a tall guy with a shaved head and one thick eyebrow that was furrowed in anger, wasn't listening. "You kids need to *keep it down!*" he yelled (sort of ironic, when you think about it), waving his pointer finger around at the four of us. "I'm staying in the apartment next door, and I've been listening to your shouting and laughing all night. I'm here on vacation, okay? I want a relaxing experience!"

His angry shouting made a weird contrast with the waves crashing against the beach behind him. The air outside was cool, and I shivered.

Harper started to say something, then stopped. I saw her take a breath and slowly let it out. When she spoke, her voice was a lot calmer than I would have been able to manage.

"I'm sorry we bothered you," she said, "but we're not

having a party or anything. We were just hanging out eating pizza and talking."

The guy looked at her, and then his gaze traveled over to Joe, standing in front of the coffee table like he was ready to jump in as soon as Harper needed backup. Then he looked at Jones, still leaning on a pillow, and me, sitting on the couch.

"*Sure* you are," he spat, glaring at each of us in turn. "I know what kids are like. I remember being your age. You probably have beer stashed somewhere, and you're all too wasted to know how loud you're being."

Now Harper looked mad. "Actually," she said, "I don't drink. Listen, we'll keep it down, but—"

The guy swung back around to face her. "You'd better," he said, "because if I get disturbed again, I'm calling the cops."

Now I stood up. "Dude," I said, pulling out my phone and glancing at it, "it's eight p.m. If this town even has a noise ordinance, it's way too early."

He glared at me again, and Harper threw up her hands in a placating gesture. "Okay," she said quickly, "okay. Never mind. We promise to keep it down."

He turned to her. "You'd better," he repeated.

"We've got it," Harper insisted. "You won't have to come over here again."

The guy nodded, a little cockily, like he'd really shown us. Then he turned away, and Harper shut the door behind him. We could hear him walking down to the next apartment, and then the beeping of the keypad and the *click* of the door opening.

Jones, Harper, Joe, and I all stared at one another in surprise.

"Wow," Jones said finally. "What the . . ."

Harper gestured to her to keep it down. "That was crazy," she said quietly, "but throwing a party would go against my UrMotel agreement with the host. I just don't want him to complain—or worse, call the cops."

"But that's nuts," I said. "We didn't do anything wrong. What would happen if he *did* complain to the host? Would you have to pay more?"

Harper shrugged. "No. At worst, I might have to leave the apartment early. But the real danger is that the host could write a bad review of me as a tenant, and then it might be really hard for me to use the UrMotel service from that point on."

Joe shook his head. "Ugh. Well, *my* review of this place just went way down."

Harper smiled sadly. "The host can't exactly guarantee your neighbors. I don't know if she even owns that apartment. He might have rented from some other site, or someone he knows."

I caught Jones shooting me a significant glance. *Should we leave?*

I coughed. "Well, listen, we should probably get going

anyway. You were tired when we left the convention hall, so you must be exhausted now. And—"

Harper was holding up her hands. "Oh, no, don't feel like—"

She was cut off by the chorus of "Uptown Funk," which suddenly started blaring from her purse.

Looking startled, she grabbed for her purse on the kitchen counter while holding up a single finger to me. "Hold on." She dug in her purse for a few seconds, the song getting more muffled, then louder, then more muffled again. "I don't know why I carry such a big purse. I can never find anything. . . ."

The song trailed off.

"Shoot," Harper hissed. She dug a little more and then pulled out a smartphone in a Wonder Woman case. When she looked at her screen, her face fell.

"Who was it?" Jones asked.

Harper groaned. "Oh, it was Matt—my boyfriend."

Jones shrugged. "Go ahead and call him back if you need to! We'll wait."

Harper bit her lip. "It's just—my phone is almost dead, and he hates it when I don't take his calls. He gets so antsy when I leave. I think—my charger is in my car still. I—" She picked up her car keys, but Jones stopped her.

"Wait," said Jones, standing up and pulling her own phone out of her pocket. "Just call him back on mine. It has plenty of juice."

Harper beamed gratefully, taking the phone and dialing. She held the phone to her ear and strolled toward the bedroom.

"Hey," she said. "Yeah, I saw . . . No! No, I just couldn't find it in my purse. I'm calling from the landline at the apartment. I'm not doing anything, really, I'm just about to go to sleep. . . ." Jones, Joe, and I all looked at one another a little awkwardly. Jones held her finger to her lips. *Why wasn't Harper telling her boyfriend about us?*

She'd strolled into the bedroom now and stood where we couldn't see her, but we could still hear her voice, suddenly dull and worn out. "Yeah . . . That sucks . . . Well, don't worry, I'll be back tomorrow by dinnertime. Yeah. I'm not sure. It dep—" She fell silent for a minute. "Okay . . . okay. I'll leave as early as I can and try to be back for lunch. Yeah. Yeah, no, it's fine. I . . . I love you, too."

Jones raised an eyebrow, and I frowned. It was strange to hear Harper—such a vibrant, fun, independent person— turning all quiet and apologetic. This *Matt* guy didn't sound like a catch at all.

Harper walked to the doorway of the bedroom. Her eyes were downcast, and she looked about a thousand miles away.

"Um," I said. "I was saying . . . we should get going."

I kind of expected Harper to argue with me, like she had when I'd suggested that we leave the first time. But now she met my eyes—hers were serious and dark—and nodded.

"Yeah. Yeah, we should all probably get some sleep. I have to get an early start tomorrow back to Pennsylvania."

We hastily packed up our stuff and made our way to the door. I opened it, and we all piled out onto the walkway. I couldn't help noticing that the windows in the apartment next door were dark now.

Guess we quieted down enough for you to get to sleep. . . .

When I turned back to my friends, Jones had put her hand on Harper's shoulder.

"It was *so* awesome to finally meet you in person," she said.

Harper's lips lifted in a small smile—a real smile. "It was great to meet you, too. I had fun today."

"Most perfect day ever!" I added, but somehow all our previous excitement had ebbed. Harper looked at me almost sadly. Were those tears in her eyes?

"Maybe we can hang out again sometime," Jones said, patting Harper's shoulder.

"I would really like that," Harper said, and wiped at the corner of her eye. "Anyway, I'm sorry, guys, I just got so tired all of a sudden. Have a safe drive back!" She waved, then slipped back inside and closed the door.

It was a quiet drive back to Bayport. Partly because we were all a little confused by Harper's behavior right before we left, and partly because Joe and Jones immediately passed out, Joe snoring loudly enough to nearly drown out the radio. I didn't mind, though. We'd had a nearly perfect day. And even though I hadn't been sure Joe would enjoy himself, I was glad he'd come.

I'd pulled off the Garden State Parkway and was following the long path of secondary roads to Jones's house, when suddenly she sat up in the passenger seat, wide awake. "Oh, no!"

She startled me enough that the car swerved a little, but I was able to correct it quickly. "What's up?" I asked, glancing at her with concern.

She groaned. "My phone," she said, holding up a smartphone in a Wonder Woman case. "We were in such a hurry to leave, I grabbed Harper's phone instead of mine. And I think she left *mine* in the bedroom."

"Oh, ugh," I murmured.

Joe suddenly sat straight up in the backseat, like the Ghost of Road Trips Past. "Whasshappening?"

"Jones accidentally took Harper's phone and left her own," I explained.

Joe moaned, but I couldn't tell whether it was in response to what I'd said.

"Tell you what," I said. "Don't worry. Grab my phone and send a text to yours to tell Harper we have her phone, and we'll be back at eight a.m. tomorrow to switch them."

"She said she was leaving early," Jones reminded me, but she picked up my phone and began typing.

"If she wants to leave earlier than that, she can text me back," I pointed out.

Then Jones groaned again—louder this time. "Oh, shoot. I have a band rehearsal tomorrow morning." She looked at me and sighed. "I can't miss it. We're starting to work on some new material."

Jones bit her lip. She always does that when she's worried.

"Don't sweat it," I told her. "Joe and I will go. You'll have your phone back before the rehearsal ends."

"Oh, Frank," she said, a huge smile on her face. "You're such a prince."

"And you're my kick-butt superhero girlfriend," I said, reaching over to take her hand.

"And I guess I'm just the dumb schlub who gets to wake up at six a.m. to go with you," said a creaky voice from the backseat. *Joe.* Right. I'd forgotten about him for a minute. "Also? Barf!"

SURPRISE! 3

JOE

THE THINGS I DO FOR MY BROTHER.

Here it is, seven thirty a.m. on a Sunday, and am I facedown in my pillow, enjoying my favorite recurring dream of growing giant antennae that allow me to control thoughts and also receive free HBO?

No, I am not.

Am I hunkered over my desk, poring over SAT prep book #428 in search of the best strategy for eliminating wrong multiple-choice answers?

Noooooooooo.

I am in a car. *Our* car. *The* car. Frank is driving (least he can do) and we are halfway through the hour-long drive back to Margate, the town where Harper's UrMotel is, to intercept her and exchange phones.

"Did she send anything yet?" Frank asked, gesturing to his phone, which lay between us in the cup holder, charging. In the next holder over was Harper's phone in its matching Wonder Woman case.

I lifted Frank's phone and looked at the screen. "Still nothing," I said.

Frank sighed. "Well, I guess we just have to hope we get there before she leaves."

We were quiet for a minute. Thinking of Harper still left a funny taste in my mouth—like there was something there that I hadn't quite figured out.

"Did you think she was weird about the comic dealer guy?" I asked.

"Von," Frank supplied. "ComiczVon."

"Whoever," I said. "Just—she ran off to avoid him, right? That's the most logical explanation. That's why she didn't come back and find us, even though we hung out in that aisle for a long time, waiting."

Frank took a minute to reply. "The thought did occur to me," he admitted finally.

"And the boyfriend," I added. "Remember? That's the excuse she gave when she ran off before Von came up to us—she had to call her boyfriend back. Maybe she saw him and got out of there before he could catch up with her."

Frank raised his eyebrows. "You could be right."

"Seems like a messed-up relationship," I added, looking at Frank for confirmation. But he was focused on the road. "She was so nervous about calling him back right away. Remember? And then she calls, and she gets all down, and she's suddenly promising to be back right away and apologizing for things that don't need apologizing for."

I paused, hoping Frank would add something. But he was silent, driving, staring out at the highway.

"That's not a relationship built on *trust*," I pointed out.

Frank just nodded again.

"Hey, plug in her phone for a few minutes," he suggested. "Mine is probably fully charged now. That way, she'll be able to use it on her way home if she needs to."

"She said she has a charger," I reminded him, but I unplugged Frank's phone and plugged in Harper's anyway.

Within thirty seconds or so, the phone began beeping—first once, then several times in a row. I picked it up and looked at the screen. "A bunch of texts are coming in."

"See?" said Frank. "Harper was right—her phone must have been nearly dead. Didn't even have enough juice to receive a text."

But I was still staring at the screen—watching text after text pop up. "Um, Frank . . ."

"What?" My brother glanced at me.

"These are all from her boyfriend," I said. "Matt. And . . . they're kind of creepy."

"What do you mean?"

I read the texts to Frank, in order. They ranged from HEY, CAN'T WAIT TO SEE YOU to WHERE R U? to WHAT ARE YOU DOING THERE? to CALL ME NOW!!!!

Frank shook his head. "Wow. I get why Harper totally changed after talking to him last night."

"Yeah." I stared at the screen. "Dude, maybe we should write back."

"We don't have her password, though," Frank pointed out.

I touched the phone to wake it up. The texts had just appeared on the home screen, but sure enough, when I wanted to go into MESSAGES to reply, it prompted me to enter the password. "Yeah, it's locked."

Frank sighed. "How many letters does it need?"

I looked up at him. "We're breaking into her phone now?"

Frank groaned. "We don't have a way to get in touch with her! She isn't responding to the text Jones sent from my phone last night, " he said, a little defensively. "And honestly, this Matt sounds like a creep. I'm worried that if we don't write back and explain, she could be headed back into a dangerous situation."

I swallowed. "You don't think . . ."

As sleuths and human beings, Frank and I were well aware that not all guys were nice to their significant others. But some guys could go pretty far in the other direction from "nice."

"We don't know," Frank said. "But I don't want to regret anything."

"True. There are nine spaces."

"Try 'Wonder Wom,' like Wonder Woman for short? It is her phone case, after all," Frank suggested.

I typed it in. "No . . . maybe another comic character?"

Frank started listing some off some that might work. But nothing did.

"Call Jones," Frank said finally. "She'll know what to do."

"But Harper has her phone," I replied.

"Yeah," said Frank after a moment, "but there should be a listing in my phone for her parents' landline. Sometimes I call her there if her phone is dead. She's supposed to be rehearsing with her band in the garage."

I called, and got to meet (via phone, anyway) Jones's charming dad, who was very excited about this article he'd read in the *New York Times* about traveling to Costa Rica. (Landline plus hard-copy newspaper subscription. Yup, Jones's parents were *parents*, all right.) Finally he put Jones on, and I explained what we were up to as quickly as I could.

"How scary are the messages?" Jones asked, her voice tight. "Like . . . he's not threatening to *hurt* her, is he?"

"No, no," I said. "But he seems angry, so we wanted to explain."

Jones let out a breath. "Okay. Well, I hope you can type fast, Joe. Here are some ideas. . . ."

My fingers flew as I tried each of Jones's comic book character suggestions in turn. We tried two, then five, then ten, then fifteen. . . .

"How are there still more characters?" I whined, my fingers shaking.

"Dude," Jones replied, "the world of comics is rich and varied. That's like saying, why are there still so many fictional detectives, or why are there so many Shakespeare characters?"

"Wait!" I cried. I'd just finished typing Jones's last suggestion—*Poison Ivy*—into the keypad, and amazingly, the screen didn't bounce back to the INCORRECT PASSWORD, TRY AGAIN screen. Instead . . .

It led me to the home screen. The phone was unlocked. "Success!" I yelled.

"Really?" Jones asked. "Huh."

"What?" I asked, clicking on MESSAGES.

"It's just interesting," Jones said. "She sees herself as a Poison Ivy type. That's cool. I'm not judging."

I typed out a quick message—HEY MAN HARPER LEFT HER PHONE WITH US BY ACCIDENT SO SHE HASN'T GOTTEN YOUR TEXTS BUT SHE'S FINE WE'RE ON OUR WAY TO RETURN HER PHONE!—and hit send. Immediately, a little DELIVERED showed up under the message. Then, within seconds, READ 7:43 A.M.

Then the little dots showed up that told me Matt was writing back.

Then the message popped up.

WHAT?? WHO THE ARE YOU??

"Uh-oh. He seems angry," I murmured.

"What?" asked Frank.

"What?" asked Jones, who was still on the line.

I read them the message as I typed a reply: I'M JUST JOE HARDY A FRIEND OF HARPER'S NO BIG WHOOP!

Dots. Immediately. And within seconds:

WHAT IS HARPER DOINMG WITH ANOTHETR GUY.

And then, before I could respond,

IF I FIDND YOU THERE YOU WILL BE SORRY.

"Oh, no," I muttered. Jones and Frank looked concerned, so I filled them in.

"You gave him your full name?" Jones asked, incredulous.

"Yes, I like to be honest," I told her. "And I figured if he wanted to, he could look me up and see I'm a stand-up guy."

"Or he could look up your street address and show up with a machete," Jones pointed out. "Seriously, you're a detective?"

"I *didn't know* it was going to go so *badly*, okay?!" I huffed, shaking my head.

"Text him back," Frank said sharply. "Tell him to calm down. You're just Harper's friend, and she'll text him when she has her phone back."

I did. But now there was no answer. And the DELIVERED message wasn't turning to READ.

"He's not checking his phone," I guessed.

"I hope that doesn't mean he's on his way somewhere," said Jones.

I was about to say something defensive about giving

him my name, when I realized that probably wasn't what Jones meant.

Matt probably knew where Harper was staying. Which meant he could be on his way there. Or maybe even on his way to intercept her when she got back to Pennsylvania.

"Jones," I said, having a sudden brainstorm, "do you have a way to check the messages on your phone remotely?"

"Um, I think so," she said. I could hear her opening a laptop, then typing. "Do you think he might try to contact her on my phone?"

"He would have the number," Frank said in a low voice. "From when she called him last night."

"But wait, I think she told him she was calling from a landline," I reminded them. "Maybe check your voice mail?"

There was silence for a few seconds as we all thought that over, and Jones kept typing on her computer. Then, what seemed like hours later but was probably only a minute or so, she said, "I'm in . . . ohhh."

"What is it?" Frank asked.

Jones responded by playing the voice mail so we could hear it.

"Seriously," a ragged male voice said, "what are you trying to do to me? I don't know where you are. I don't know why you're not answering your phone. You're calling me from strange numbers. What am I supposed to think?" And then a second later, louder, nearly screaming: "WHAT AM I SUPPOSED TO THINK, HARPER?!"

"Oh, man," Frank whispered.

"Where are you?" Jones asked urgently.

"Only about ten minutes away," Frank said. "We're not far now."

"Good," Jones replied. "Call me the minute you get there, okay? I'll tell my dad to grab me. I hope he didn't talk your ear off about Costa Rica."

"No," I said. "It was all kind of interesting."

"Good. Talk soon."

Jones hung up, and I looked at Frank. He looked as freaked out as I felt.

"I hope Harper's okay," I said quietly, stating the obvious.

Frank nodded. "Me too," he said. "This is going to be a really long ten minutes."

When we pulled into the apartment complex, everything looked normal from the outside. Lots of people looked like they were in the process of leaving, rolling suitcases to their cars and loading them in.

"There's Harper's car," Frank said, his voice thick with relief.

"Oh, thank God," I murmured, noting the little blue sports car. "She's still here."

"Let's just hope she's alone," Frank added, pulling the car into a space.

We hopped out of the car and ran to the gate, where I suddenly remembered: we didn't know the security code. I took a quick glance through Harper's phone but couldn't find anything obvious in her messages or e-mails. . . .

"Let's just buzz her," Frank said. "Hopefully she'll answer."

So we did—we buzzed apartment 2F once, then twice, then just over and over and over.

Frank met my seriously freaked-out look. "She's not answering. This isn't good," he said.

"Maybe she's indisposed," I said, and Frank looked confused. "Maybe she's in the shower or trapped under a heavy piece of furniture or something," I explained.

Frank sighed. "That seems . . . unlikely."

I glanced past the gate at the complex. Most of the people who'd been loading their cars when we pulled in had left already. "Maybe we just have to explain our situation to the next person to come out," I suggested. "When they see how worried we are, they'll let us in. . . ."

"You think?" asked Frank, nodding to a person coming through the lobby.

Oh, man. It was the guy. The same guy who'd been in the apartment next to Harper's, who'd threatened to call the cops on our "party."

"Oh, no," I muttered.

As he got closer, he didn't exactly look thrilled to see us, either. "You again?" he sneered.

"Listen," said Frank, putting on his "no-nonsense" tone. "I know we didn't meet under the best of circumstances, but you have to help us. We're worried about our friend Harper.

We accidentally switched phones with her, so we came to bring this one back, but meanwhile she's not answering the buzz or responding to any of our messages. We want to make sure she's okay. Could you let us in?"

The guy looked from Frank to me, still sneering, but then shook his head. "All right," he said. "I'll let you in, but just for a minute or so to check on her. And I'm certainly going to mention all of this in my review. I *thought* these were family-friendly apartments, but people should know about the undesirable tenants. . . ."

By this time, he'd swung the gate open, so we ignored the rest of his rant and bolted by him. In seconds we'd run through the lobby and out to the patio, then up the stairs. We thundered down the walkway and squealed to a stop outside apartment 2F.

The door was ajar.

I was beginning to feel an icy sensation creep up my spine. With the lack of response from her; all her strange, scared behavior the day before; this psycho boyfriend; and now, an open door to her apartment, it was getting harder and harder to believe that Harper was fine.

Frank shoved the door open and we both ran in. The apartment was silent, and there was nothing immediately notable about the living room. Frank ran into the bedroom. "Oh, man," he groaned.

I followed him in and saw what he meant.

There was stuff strewn everywhere. The mattress had been

pulled off the box spring and lay flopped to the side. Harper's suitcase was still there—but it was open, and all her belongings and clothing had been thrown around the room.

There was no sign of Harper.

"Hey, Frank," I said, as I noticed something black peeking out from beneath a T-shirt. It was Jones's cell phone. I picked it up and handed it to Frank.

He hit the button to illuminate the screen. Then he quickly typed in a code.

"You know Jones's password?" I asked, feeling a weird mixture of impressed and grossed out.

"Yeah," he said, barely looking at me. "It's 'Samson,' for Abigail Samson, the woman who directed the *Dagger Girl* movie. *Phew*."

"What is it?" I asked.

"No new voice mails since Jones checked," he said. "Maybe he's calmed down?"

That's when we heard pounding footsteps on the stairs, moving onto the walkway.

"Did we close the door behind us when we walked in?" I hissed.

Frank looked helpless. "I can't remember."

Then we heard someone yelling in the living room . . . the same ragged voice we'd heard in the voice mail. "HARPER?!"

Then more heavy footsteps. Then a face peeked into the bedroom—short dark hair; wide red face.

"WHO THE HECK ARE *YOU*??"

MAD MATT

4

FRANK

JEALOUS BOYFRIENDS ARE ALL THE SAME. It's a pattern Joe and I have seen before. Deeply insecure, worried that their girlfriend might find someone better . . . so they get possessive and say they "have to" keep track of her every minute. It starts with wanting to know her whereabouts at every moment, and it can escalate into wanting to control where she goes and who she spends time with, until the poor girl is practically this guy's prisoner. It's not a good scenario. Sometimes, when someone intervenes early on, these guys learn to deal with their insecurity in healthier ways. The worst ones turn into criminals.

That's why it was important to handle this dude very carefully.

"Dude, don't worry, we're no one," blurted Joe.

Not what I would have started with . . .

The dude stepped forward. "'No one' who has Harper's phone," he pointed out. "'No one' who was WITH HER LAST NIGHT!"

"Just in a group!" I said, holding up my hands to look as harmless as possible. "Look, Harper is a friend of my *girlfriend's*. The three of us were just eating pizza and talking. But when you called, Harper's phone was nearly dead, so my girlfriend loaned her hers. Unfortunately, we left right after that and no one remembered to switch the phones back."

The dude took in a breath through his nose—good sign—and straightened up a little, his eyes darting back and forth from me to Joe.

"Hey, let's restart here?" Joe said. "I'm the guy who texted you. Joe." He gestured at me with his elbow. "That's Frank. And I'm thinking you're Matt."

He took in another breath and nodded. "When did you leave?" Matt asked, his voice sounding a little more normal.

"Around nine," Joe replied. "Harper seemed really tired, and she said she wanted to leave early this morning."

"Actually—" I jumped in, thinking I'd mention the guy next door who broke up the party with his complaints. But then I thought better of it. Somehow it didn't seem like a good idea to let this guy think it was such a wild party that the neighbors wanted to call the cops. "Actually, we've been trying to reach her," I said instead. "We were hoping we'd get here before she left, so we could give her phone back."

Matt wasn't looking at either of us now. He was sort of staring into a middle distance, like he could see something there that no one else could. I wondered if it was part of his calming-down ritual. "She didn't leave," he said suddenly, looking up at me, and I could swear his voice broke a little. "At least, she didn't come home. Her car's still out there."

I nodded, trying to make my expression sympathetic. "We just got in here and started looking for her when you showed up," I explained.

He glanced up, looking around the small apartment. "Did you find anything?"

"No," Joe said. "But . . . the door was open when we got here." He paused. "And the bedroom is pretty messed up, as you can see."

Matt looked around at the mattress and thrown-around clothes, seeming to see them for the first time. "Oh God," he said. "You think . . ."

I watched his face. He really did look worried. "Maybe Harper had some uninvited guests," I said quietly.

Matt looked around the room—the bed, the suitcase. Then he backed out of the bedroom and walked somewhere else. Joe and I exchanged a glance and followed. When we caught up, he was standing in the doorway to the small apartment bathroom.

"None of her stuff is unpacked," he said, pointing at the

sink, which held only a toothbrush. "She takes forever to get ready. Has a ton of products, hair, makeup. She usually carries a little bag of stuff, but it looks like she never took it out." He turned and looked at us. "That means she didn't get herself ready this morning."

That's a bad sign. I glanced at Joe and could see he was thinking the same.

"The shower's not wet," I said, suddenly realizing. "So unless she left really early, she didn't shower, either."

"This is not good," Matt muttered.

"Let's not jump to conclusions," said Joe. "Maybe she got up and wanted to leave right away. But there was something wrong with her car, so she left to . . . take the train? Or a bus?"

"And left her stuff?" Matt pointed out. I'd been thinking the same thing but hadn't wanted to say anything, for fear of upsetting him. "And *trashed her own room*?" The tension was rising in his voice.

Joe sighed. "Is there any reason she wouldn't come home?" he asked. "Maybe . . ."

Matt shook his head strongly. "No. No, she always comes home." He paused, moaned, and put his face into his hands. "Oh God, I'm sorry, Harper. Just let her be okay. . . ."

I looked at Joe. His face said: *Sorry?* I gave a tiny nod.

"Um, what are you sorry about?" I asked.

Matt rubbed his face with his hands and, after a few seconds, looked up at me. His eyes were red. "We had a stupid fight," he said. "Right before she left for the convention. It's had me on edge all day yesterday and today."

I felt a sudden ray of hope. "A fight?" I asked. "Well, is there any way Harper could have been mad enough to not come home?" I had a sudden vision of her walking on the beach, coffee in hand, trying to figure the whole thing out. That still left the question of what happened to the bedroom, but maybe she'd been mad enough to trash it herself?

Matt began shaking his head almost immediately, though, dashing my hope. "No. Harper always comes home, like I said. She gets mad, she goes somewhere to think it over, she comes home, I say I'm sorry. We talked on the phone last night, and she was fine. We've been talking about getting married. I'm in this for the long haul." He rubbed his hand over his hair. "It was just a stupid fight, like any couple has."

I could tell from Joe's face that he was thinking the same thing I was: "stupid fight like any couple has" didn't seem to match up with Matt's crazy texts, and how obsessed he was with Harper coming home right away. Even the phone call he'd mentioned had seemed upsetting to Harper, although I didn't want to let Matt know we'd been around to witness that call. I realized then that Matt had said, I'm *in this for the long haul*, not We're *in this*. Was it possible that he and Harper were on different pages?

Maybe Harper had felt trapped?

"Why don't we sit down and talk a little?" Joe suggested,

gesturing at the couch and floor cushions, still spread out where they'd been the night before.

Matt looked at him a little suspiciously, then shrugged and sat down on the couch. "I'm not sure what else to do," he admitted.

"What was the fight about?" I asked, sitting down on a cushion on the floor.

Matt sighed. "It's hard to remember," he said. "We've been fighting about a lot of dumb stuff lately. I know I didn't want her to go to the convention."

"You didn't?" Joe asked. "Why?"

Matt scowled. "She's always taking off for 'comic book this' or 'convention that'—all things that take place hours away from where we live, that I'm not interested in." He sighed again. "Would it be too much to ask to spend one weekend with my girlfriend? To maybe spend some time with people she'd be willing to introduce me to?"

"You haven't met any of her comic book friends?" Joe asked.

"Why would I?" Matt asked. "I don't care about comics. And she's so secretive about them—she won't even tell me their names."

I looked at Joe. Who to believe? Was Harper really trying to conceal friends from Matt, or was he just offended that she had her own interests, like so many jealous boyfriends we'd seen?

"Anyway," Matt said, "we were getting close to working it out."

"What makes you say that?" I asked.

"When we talked about it, Harper was arguing with me less. She seemed to understand that if we're going to make a life together, we have to focus on each other."

Did she think that? I wondered. *Or did she just stop arguing with you because she knew she was going to run away?*

"Is there anyone you can call?" Joe asked suddenly, startling me out of my thoughts. "A close friend, a family member? Someone Harper might tell if she . . . had a change of plans?"

"How would she have contacted anyone?" Matt asked, giving Joe a challenging look. "You had her phone, and she left yours here. No calls, right?"

Right. I looked at Joe like, *Well?*

Joe shrugged. "I don't know, exactly, okay? But there are other ways to communicate with people. Maybe she went for a walk and used a pay phone, or got online somehow. Either way, it's starting to feel like we need to call the police. And before we do that, maybe we should check in with her family, make sure there's nothing we don't know."

Matt's eyes widened at the word "police." And I felt a little jolted too. But I couldn't argue with Joe's logic. If something *had* happened to Harper, they'd need to be involved.

Matt pulled a smartphone out of his pants pocket and pushed the button to turn on the screen. Then he started clicking through menus. "I can call her aunt Patty," he said. "She's all the family Harper's got—she raised her from the age of eight. Harper's parents had their issues. They've both passed on now."

He pressed a button to dial.

"Can you put her on speaker?" Joe asked.

Matt looked a little annoyed but nodded, pulled the phone away from his ear, and pushed the speaker button.

"Hello?" an older female voice answered.

"Hey, Patty, this is Matt," Matt replied. "Listen, have you heard from Harper?"

"*Harper?*" Patty asked, sounding as surprised as if Matt had asked whether she'd heard from Big Bird. "No. Why?"

"She hasn't come home today," Matt explained. "And actually—well, I came down here to meet her at the place she was staying, and her car and stuff are here, but she's nowhere to be found."

There was silence at the other end of the line—just breathing. It lasted a few seconds. "I haven't heard from her," Patty said. "But you know how she is, Matt. That girl's a little wild."

Matt sighed, and a flash of annoyance moved across his face, like he'd had this conversation before—and didn't like it.

"Yeah, yeah. You don't know nothing, though?"

"I don't," Patty said. "But I bet she'll turn up, and she'll have some crazy story to tell."

Matt shook his head. "All right. Thanks, Patty. Bye." And he clicked the hang-up button before Joe or I could say anything.

"What does she mean, 'wild'?" I asked.

Matt groaned. "That's what Patty always says. Harper was a tough kid to raise, I guess—she had a mind of her own, she was always taking off and getting into trouble. But she's been growing out of that, getting ready to settle down with me." He paused, looking thoughtful. "We've been saving up for a down payment on a house. Something must have . . ."

Matt trailed off as the sound of footsteps on the stairs, then the walkway, grew louder and louder. Someone might be headed for this apartment. He stood up.

"Harper . . . ?" he called.

But when the door banged open, it definitely was not Harper who stood there.

"Who the hell are all of *you*?!" asked an older woman wearing white capri pants and a T-shirt with a rhinestoned flamingo on it. Carefully styled orange-tinted hair winged out from her head like a crown.

Then she pulled something out of her pocket and pointed it at us.

It was a tiny pistol—only slightly bigger than the palm of her hand. It had a shiny pearled handle. Guess she liked sparkly things.

"Um, hello. I'm Joe. And who are you?" Joe asked.

This was not a great turn of events.

Surprisingly, Matt stood up with a smile on his face, looking happy to see her. "I'm Matt. Do you know where Harper is?" he asked eagerly.

The woman scowled at him, the lines around her mouth deepening into ravines. If I had to guess, I'd say this woman was a smoker. "I'm Geraldine," she replied in a raspy voice, jabbing the gun in his direction. "I own this place. And if I'm not mistaken, I have the gun, so I get to ask the questions!"

"Look, we're just friends of Harper's," I said quickly. "You know, your guest, Harper. We came here today to give her phone back, and found her missing."

Geraldine pursed her lips. "Missing? Really?" She lowered the gun and shoved it back into her pocket. I hoped the thing had the safety on. "Sorry about that. I hate to get off on the wrong foot, but you can't be too careful these days. World is going to the dogs."

I didn't know what to say to that, but fortunately, Joe did. "So you own this place."

Geraldine nodded. Her hair barely moved. "I own five places, actually. Three apartments here in this complex and two in the Sandpiper on the Atlantic City boardwalk. Anyway, crime is up these days. I've even heard there've been abductions in the area. That's why I invest in top-of-the-line security. Automated system, video cameras, the whole nine yards. Actually, I just got a complaint from another tenant that two weirdos have been hanging around, asking for access to the building."

I looked at Joe. *That's us—and the complainy guy.* But before we could say anything, Geraldine suddenly turned to the door she'd walked through and pulled it toward her. "What on earth!"

Matt, Joe, and I all looked at one another. "Is something wrong?" Matt asked.

"You bet something's wrong," Geraldine replied, reaching into her pocket (not the one where the gun was) and pulling out an old-fashioned flip-style cell phone. "Someone ripped the dang chain lock off the door. This apartment's been broken into. I'm calling the police!"

"And then Geraldine showed up," Joe said. He sounded a little monotone, but I couldn't blame him, really—we were telling the same story for the fifth time, sitting in an interrogation room at the Margate police station. The two police detectives who were listening to us now exchanged a glance, and one, Detective McGill, made a note. "She said the chain lock had been ripped off the door, and she called the police."

McGill kept writing, and the other detective, Gomez, leveled a penetrating glare at us.

"Just to recap," she said, "you guys had never met Mr. Driscoll before?"

Mr. Driscoll was Matt, we'd found out. And the police seemed super interested in learning all they could about him.

"Never," I said. "We didn't even think he'd be there. We were just there to check on Harper."

"Even though you'd just met her the day before?" Gomez prodded.

We nodded. "We wanted to give her back her phone, remember," Joe said. "And when she didn't answer the buzz, we were worried about her."

McGill wrote for a few more seconds. Then he stopped, and he and Gomez looked at each other.

"Okay," McGill said, closing up his notebook. "Thank you, boys. I think that will do it."

"That's it?" asked Joe, eyebrows raised.

"Yes," said Gomez. "You're free to go."

"After all that?" Joe pressed. Then he seemed to remember he was kind of challenging a police officer, and added a big white smile.

McGill stood up. "You boys may have an interesting record, but it's a clean one," he explained. "And the security footage from the convention center and the apartment building backs up your story. We also spoke to your father by phone, and he told us what time you got home last night and left this morning."

For many people, the fact that police officers from a strange town had called and spoken to their parents about their possible involvement in a crime would have been the thing that jumped out about McGill's statements.

Not for me.

"Security cameras!" I repeated, slapping my hand against the table. "That's right! Geraldine said they were all over the apartments."

Gomez looked bored. "Yup."

"So they must show what happened," I said, looking eagerly from Gomez to McGill. "Do you know who took Harper? If anyone took Harper?"

Gomez and McGill looked at each other, and I could see the conversation playing out on their faces: *We don't have to tell them anything.* (Gomez.) *Yeah, but they seem harmless. And they're worried about their friend.* (McGill.)

"*Well*," McGill said finally, playing a little drum solo on top of his notebook, "here's the thing. The footage is kind of useless on that front."

"What?" asked Joe, brow furrowed.

"Yeah, how?" I added. "Did the camera malfunction?"

"No, it's actually much more irritating than that," McGill said, frowning. "There was a plant blocking the view of the camera on the walkway, and the lobby cameras show nothing unusual."

A plant? I thought, trying to make sense of that. *Did someone block the camera on purpose, then? Or was it just a coincidence?*

I looked at Joe and could tell he was mulling all this over too. It was a lot to take in.

And we still don't know where Harper is, or whether she's safe.

Gomez stood up. "Listen, you boys should go home and get some rest," she said. "Let us handle this. We've got it."

When we didn't move, McGill shot us a sympathetic look. "Don't worry," he said. "We're taking your friend's disappearance very seriously. We've had a couple other people disappear from UrMotel rooms recently, so this is part of an even bigger investigation. Rest assured, no rock will go unturned in our search for your friend."

Joe and I shared a look. This might be part of something bigger? That was not reassuring.

Officer Gomez must have picked up on our concern, because she quickly added, "They've all had reasons to want to disappear, though, so we're not even sure if Harper's case is related. She could even turn up later today."

Reasons to disappear. I thought back to what Patty had said—about Harper being 'wild.'" And I remembered Matt's crazy voice in the messages he'd left for Harper.

Did Harper have reasons to want to disappear?

"What will you do next?" Joe asked. Even as long as we'd been there, he seemed, like me, reluctant to leave.

"First we'll interview more people," McGill said. "Try to do some more research into Harper's life, starting with her phone. Then forensics. Hopefully that will give us a lead."

I looked at Joe and nodded. None of that was surprising, but it was comforting in a way to know the police at least had a plan. As it was, every sleuthing cell in my body was freaking out at the idea of leaving Margate with a case unsolved. But we had to, right? The police were on it.

After a second, we stood up.

McGill and Gomez stood up too. "I'll walk you out," Gomez said, gesturing toward the door.

She led us down a hallway that passed by another

interrogation room. Inside, through the window on the door, I could see Matt. He looked flushed and uncomfortable.

Gomez saw me looking. "Oh, don't bother waiting for your new friend," she warned. "Mr. Driscoll isn't going home any time soon!"

"He isn't?" asked Joe. "Why, is he a suspect?"

Gomez shook her head. "You know I can't answer that," she said. I watched her glance back with contempt at the room that held Matt.

I remembered how tense Harper had been last night when she saw he'd called . . . and how completely she'd changed when she hung up with Matt.

Did he do something to Harper?

JOE

THERE ARE TWO WORDS THAT SHOULD never be used to describe studying for the SAT:

"*Fun.*"

"*Easy.*"

Especially when you're me, Joe Hardy, and you're kind of in the middle of a case that is unsolved and *maybe* seems impossible. That's when my brain goes nuts with every possible explanation, motivation, secret method, wild theory . . . or it tries to, at least.

The day after we got back from Margate, my brain kept being rudely interrupted from focusing on my practice by SAT questions. I read:

15. As used in line 18, "claim" most clearly means

A. to declare one's own
B. an entitlement
C. to maintain
D. a spoiled clam

But what my brain understood was:

15. Shortly after waking up at her UrMotel, Harper heard a disturbance outside. It was

A. the mean neighbor guy, with a baseball bat
B. a totally friendly guy she'd met at Comic-Con, asking her to get breakfast
C. Matt, in some kind of psychotic rage
D. a talking seagull, wanting to discuss politics

There's always one answer you can eliminate off the bat, they tell me. Rumor has it it's usually D.

Anyway, I was not getting very far in my studies. I was finding it very hard to concentrate, even though Frank and Jones were in our living room, doing research on the case so I didn't have to. That's how Frank described it, anyway.

With a sigh, I closed my laptop and stood up. I'd just tell Frank and Jones this one thing, I promised myself. Then I'd study the whole rest of the day.

Jones spotted me immediately, and they both looked up from the desktop computer to shoot me frustrated looks.

"What are you doing out here?!" Frank demanded. "You're supposed to be studying. Get back in there, bro! We've got this."

"It's just . . ." Faced with all that pushback, my brilliant observation suddenly seemed less important. "I was thinking," I went on. "Maybe Harper met someone at Comic-Con that we don't know about. She got there before us, right?"

Jones rolled her eyes, which I thought was somewhat uncalled for. "Way ahead of you, Joe. Don't worry, we're looking at all possible angles."

I have to admit, it didn't feel great to see someone else doing active sleuthing with Frank. We'd both dated girls before, but before now, no girlfriend had taken over as co-sleuth on any case.

So I ignored her and looked at Frank. "Did the police call?"

He shook his head. "No, Joe. Go back to studying."

"So there's no news?" I pulled my sweatshirt sleeves over my hands and crossed my arms, feeling restless.

"No." Frank sighed. "Seriously, Joe, nothing is happening. Go study!"

I nodded, like I understood, then took a step back toward my room. But I couldn't do it.

"I can't *concentrate*," I whined, turning back around.

"Joe, I know it's hard," Frank said in his calm, measured

voice. "But we decided to trust the Margate police to handle this, remember?"

I groaned.

"You have to study, anyway," Frank reminded me. "The police are on it. And we're doing some investigating. Just go focus on your practice tests."

"Think of the Bayport police, though," I said, thinking through all our old cases. "I mean, they *try*, but . . . What if the Margate police are like that? And if they are, can they really be 'on it'?"

Frank just sighed again. "Joe . . ."

"You can't say they are," I pointed out. "Because you know they might not be. Police are fine and all, but they miss things. And what if Harper is in danger?"

Frank and Jones looked at the computer screen. "Right now," Frank said, "we have no reason to believe that she is."

"But . . ." I stepped into the living room, peering over their shoulders at the screen. "What *was* on her phone? Anything helpful?"

But wait, a person might think, *I thought they gave Harper's phone to the police in Margate.* And we did. But this wasn't our first time at the rodeo, so we took certain precautions before handing it over.

Frank and I always travel with a small, powerful flash drive. In our car on the way to the Margate police station, before the cops even knew Harper's phone existed, I'd copied some of its contents onto the drive while Frank drove.

We didn't have a ton of time (small towns, man), so I'd had to limit it to only messages, calls, and e-mails that had been exchanged over the last week.

Now Frank had the drive plugged into the family desktop, and he and Jones were poring over the contents.

Jones shook her head. "Not really," she said. "She and Matt had kind of a messed-up relationship, they fought a lot, but we knew that. There aren't any threats here or mentions of any specific incidents where she felt threatened."

"I mean, Matt clearly had a temper," added Frank, "but we kinda knew that from spending half an hour with him."

I stared at the screen, quickly reading through some day-to-day texts between Harper and Matt. Frank and Jones were right: some messages were testy, but it was nothing that couldn't be explained by a bad mood.

"Are there texts from anyone you didn't expect?" I asked. "A new suspect, maybe?"

Jones tapped the corner of the screen. "There's one mystery texter—a Jersey number, not in Harper's contacts. They're all about an appointment that Harper kept putting off."

I shrugged. "That could just be her doctor, maybe? Or her dentist? Maybe she's just putting off her yearly cleaning in the hopes of making it look like she's been flossing all along. We've all been there, am I right?"

Frank rolled his eyes. "Speak for yourself, Joe. I floss every night."

"You would," I muttered, still reading the screen. "But

actually, why would her doctor be in Jersey? And it looks like she has a couple doctors identified in her contacts, and this didn't come from them."

"It could be anything, though," Jones said. "Maybe it was a therapist, or a career counselor, or a job interview. The point is, it doesn't seem like a motive for anyone to hurt her."

I sighed. "I guess so."

Frank turned around to look at me. "Go back and study, Joe," he said. "I told you, we've got this."

Frowning, I obeyed this time and shuffled reluctantly back to my room. I opened up my laptop and tried to focus on my practice test.

16. Harper was secretly mixed up with:
    A. the Mafia
    B. a drug dealer
    C. a cult
    D. a very nice dermatologist

I shook my head to clear it, which only made me sneeze violently.

"Ugh," I muttered, making a mental note to dust my room. I reached into the pocket of my sweatshirt, thinking maybe I'd find a balled-up tissue.

But I didn't. What I found was better.

"Guys! *Guys!*" I ran into the living room, waving what I'd found.

"Dude," Frank said, looking up at me with his nose wrinkled. "Get a tissue!"

"Sorry." I ran into the bathroom, grabbed a tissue, wiped, and tossed it—then ran back out. "But I found something!"

"What's that?" Jones asked.

I held up the item from my pocket again—a business card. "The guy we met at Comic-Con," I reminded them. "The guy Harper seemed to be avoiding." I looked at the card. "ComiczVon. Remember? Does the number 201-555-3549 sound familiar?"

Jones stared at the screen. "That's it," she said. "That's the number that was texting Harper about the meeting!"

I threw my hands in the air. "Change of plans, then!" I yelled. "We have a suspect! We're driving back to Atlantic City!"

Jones and Frank looked briefly excited—but then they looked at each other and their expressions suddenly turned guilty.

"But, Joe," said Frank. "You really should study. . . ."

"Look," I said, putting my arms down and putting on my best *I'm serious* face. "I know you guys mean well, but the truth is, I'm never going to be able concentrate on some practice test until I know Harper's safe."

I could see their expressions softening.

"And, Frank," I added, "you were there when we talked to the police. I'm afraid they're going to look for the easiest answer—either Matt did something to Harper, or Harper took off herself."

Frank looked thoughtful, but Jones raised a finger.

"But what about Occam's razor?" she asked. "You know—the theory that the simplest answer is usually the right one."

"Sometimes it is," I agreed, "But a lot of times, it's *not*. Frank and I know that better than anybody."

Frank let out a breath through his nose. "Joe's right," he said. "A lot of the cases we've worked on have been, well, complicated."

I nodded. "See? Now, are you guys going to sit there and argue with me, or are you going to get in the car and help me solve this case so I can focus on studying?"

Frank looked at Jones beseechingly. Jones shook her head.

"All right," she said after a few seconds, "I'll help. But only on one condition."

"Name it," I said.

She pointed at my pj pants. "You have to put on some real pants."

Frank laughed. "I'll go fill Mom in on what's going on while you do."

A couple of hours later, I was wearing a pair of clean-ish jeans and sitting in Frank's car, watching a picnic area in a park outside Atlantic City. Jones was in the backseat, her laptop on her lap.

"Tell him we're here, and the package is under the bench," Frank instructed from the driver's seat.

Jones typed out a message on her keyboard. Using

information from Harper's phone, Frank had found an app that would allow us to send texts from Jones's laptop that would look like they came from Harper's phone. For the last hour or so, we'd been corresponding with ComiczVon, aka Von, the guy we'd met at the convention. Posing as Harper, Jones had set up a meeting in this park.

Now we were just waiting for him to show up.

It soon became clear from our texts that Von was very concerned about something Harper owed him. We had no idea what it was. Money? Some kind of rare comic book? Something illegal? (Harper had seemed like a girl on the up-and-up to me, but hey, if there's one thing sleuthing teaches you, it's that everyone has secrets.) Von never threatened Harper, but he kept talking about getting this thing she owed him, so Jones-as-Harper had finally said she'd bring it today. Von had instructed her to put it under a particular bench. So we'd tied up a little parcel in brown paper. The parcel actually contained one of Aunt Trudy's famous banana breads, because everyone loves banana bread, and if all went well, we could snack on it while discussing what Von wanted with Harper.

Besides, maybe the thing Harper owed him *was* banana bread. Unlikely, but you never know.

"Is that him?" Frank asked suddenly.

A smallish guy was chaining up his bike to a bike rack about twenty yards from the bench, in a little copse of trees.

"That's him," Jones confirmed. "He's even wearing the same military jacket."

This was true. But despite the tough-guy jacket, Von looked pretty diminutive and nonthreatening in the light of day. As he stepped into the light, his distinctive blue-dyed buzz cut became visible. He was wearing a Simpsons T-shirt, a pair of black jeans, and Converse sneakers that were covered with Day-Glo Batman symbols. Also, he'd ridden his bike here: not exactly a popular getaway vehicle for hardened criminals.

"What is he up to?" I murmured.

He walked from the bike rack over to the bench, looking around as though he expected someone to attack at any moment. When he came close enough to spot the parcel, a look of utter relief came over his face, and he sped up.

As he knelt down and reached out to claim the package, Frank and I leaped into action, bolting out of the car and running over to corner him.

"Hey, Von!" Frank yelled out.

"*You two,*" he muttered, looking from Frank to me as we walked closer. I guessed he was disappointed to see us instead of Harper. "What are you, her bodyguards or something?"

"Who?" I asked, just wanting to make sure we were all on the same page.

"*Harper,*" he replied. "Of course. The reason we're all here."

Frank raised an eyebrow at him. "Why would she need a bodyguard?" he asked.

Looking frustrated, Von huffed. "You tell me!" he said. "I'm just trying to get what she owes me. I'm not looking to hurt anyone."

Frank and I exchanged a glance, and I reached for the parcel and began unwrapping it. "Okay," I said. "Two questions, then . . . One, what does Harper owe you? And two, do you like banana bread?"

Von liked banana bread very much, it turns out. Like most people.

He relaxed a bit as we chatted and it became clear that Frank, Jones (who emerged from the car after a few minutes), and I just wanted to talk to him. He explained that he'd met Harper on the InkWorld forum, and they spent months flirting online. He thought it was pretty serious, and they soon began making plans to meet in person. But Harper always backed out at the last minute. And before they could meet up, Harper asked Von for a loan, claiming she needed it to pay for some medicine.

"I gave it to her," Von said, reaching for his second piece of banana bread. "I realize now that was really naive of me. But at the time, I really thought she might have feelings for me. I thought we had a future together. And she said she needed the money for medication! I thought I was doing the right thing."

"You sent it to her online?" Jones asked.

Von nodded. "Yeah, through an app she told me about. Once I sent it, there was no way to get it back, and no record that I'd even sent it. It was listed on my bank records as a purchase."

He spent months, he said, waiting for Harper to offer to pay him back, and hopelessly waiting for her to agree to meet in person. But finally he wised up and realized he'd been had. He said he felt silly for being so gullible and didn't want revenge—he just wanted his money back.

"I was starting to realize she lied about everything," he explained. "As time went on, she got careless—she'd tell me one thing, then forget, then tell me something totally different. She thanked me for sending the money so she could fix her car, and I was like, what? You said it was for medicine." He shook his head. "She'd seem to confuse me with other guys and start talking to me about stories they'd shared with her. Then, a couple of weeks ago, I got this private message on InkWorld."

Frank's eyes widened. "From who?"

"From some guy," Von said, "named DarkKnight. Or at least, that was his screen name. Anyway, he said he'd been talking to Harper for a long time, and he'd loaned her money too. But one day she messed up and sent him a message she meant to send me." He laughed bitterly. "He realized she'd played both of us. And probably a ton of other guys."

Jones looked stunned. "Do you know that for sure?" she asked. "Do you have usernames, or even real names. . . ."

"I have a whole list of usernames I could give you," Von said. "At last count, it was over ten guys. I don't know what she needed the money for, but she sure got a lot of it. All of it raised by tricking people through the InkWorld messaging service."

Von got on his phone and forwarded an e-mail to Jones with a whole list of usernames. Jones looked at Frank and shook her head, and I could tell what she was thinking: *That's a whole list of potential suspects. People with a pretty big grudge against Harper.*

We were about done with the banana bread by then, and it was getting dark. We thanked Von for the information, and Jones apologized for misleading him about the money.

"There's something else you should know," Frank said to Von. "Harper went missing from her UrMotel room yesterday morning, and we're trying to find out what happened to her."

Von's face fell. "What? That's terrible. What are the cops saying? What do you think happened her?"

None of us said anything. Then it dawned on him, his eyes became wide and panicked.

"I didn't do anything to her," he said. "I couldn't hurt a fly. I'm a vegetarian, for heaven's sake! I just wanted to meet her to ask her pay me back."

I was still a little on edge. Just because someone seems nice doesn't mean they're not guilty—a lesson Frank and I had learned the hard way more than once.

I put on my best *I mean business* face.

"Look," I said, "you seem like a nice guy, but sometimes horrible guys are able to seem like nice guys, understand?"

Von nodded.

"Did you do anything to Harper?" I growled. "You said you just wanted the money back, but maybe you felt the need to scare her. Maybe you got mad at her, and it just got out of hand. Maybe you didn't intend to hurt her."

"No way. Really." Von protested. "I understand that it looks like Harper was a victim of somebody but it wasn't me. I'm a victim too. I'll do anything I can to help you find her, though. She did some weird things, but she deserves to be safe."

I glanced at Frank. He nodded almost imperceptibly: *He seems legit.*

"Okay, Von," I said. "Sorry. I just needed . . ."

Von shook his head. "No, I get it," he said. "I had a motive. And you need the truth."

We said good-bye to Von as he headed back to his bike, unlocked it, and pedaled off into the darkening night.

"I don't think he did it," Frank said, "but he sure opened up a whole side of Harper that I didn't know existed."

"Me either." Jones looked thoughtful as she watched Von disappear. "But there's a way for us to learn more."

She ran back to the car and opened the back door.

"What are you doing?" Frank called as we followed her to the car.

Jones was already in the backseat, opening up her laptop. The overhead light illuminated her face as she stared into the screen and began typing.

"I think," she said, "it's time to hack into Harper's InkWorld account."

A FEW QUESTIONS

6

FRANK

"**Y**OU THINK YOU KNOW SOMEONE . . ."
Jones let her voice trail off as she shook
her head and stared out the window of the
Supreme Diner of Vernon, New Jersey.
We'd stopped to get some pancakes, plus
take advantage of their free Wi-Fi and check out Harper's
InkWorld account.

It hadn't been hard to guess her password. Like her
phone's password, it started with "Poison Ivy"—but here,
she'd added her birthday, which Jones already knew: 0423.
We'd been reading through her private messages for about
half an hour. It was wild—she was like another person
online. She'd been lying to at least thirteen different guys
from around the country—Von just happened to be the one

who lived closest. And she'd collected thousands of dollars from them.

"What could she have needed the money for?" I asked out loud, poking at the crumby remains of my pancakes. "Her car was a few years old. Her clothes didn't seem particularly fancy. She was living with Matt in an inexpensive part of the country."

Joe was building some kind of leaning tower with the remains of his silver dollars. "It seems like she was saving it for something," he said. "Maybe the house Matt mentioned? He said they were saving up for a down payment."

I dropped my fork. "You think Matt knew?" I asked.

"I guess it's possible," Jones said. "Like, she was doing it with his blessing?"

"Or maybe at his *urging*," I amended. "He seems . . . angry. Maybe he thought these guys had it coming?"

"But he seemed jealous, too," Jones pointed out. "Would a jealous guy encourage his girlfriend to flirt with strangers?"

"Just online," Joe said. "She never had to meet them in person . . . he never had to picture her with them. It was all on-screen."

I leaned back in the booth, stretching my arms above my head, which is how I do my best thinking.

"Maybe he did know, or he encouraged it, and then she and Matt had a big fight," Jones suggested. Joe and I leaned in closer, taken in by the theory. It definitely seemed plausible. "Maybe she took the money. Maybe she had it on her at the

UrMotel. Maybe she mentioned it to someone, and . . ."

We were startled by a sudden shrill tone. Something was vibrating in my pocket. My phone! I'd almost forgotten I had it on me.

I grabbed it and answered. "Hello?"

"Frank?"

It was my mom. "Hey, Mom. Sorry we haven't called. . . . We're heading home in, like, ten minutes or so—"

But she seemed impatient. "No, Frank, it's not about . . . Well, actually I'm calling because some police officers just showed up at the house."

"Police officers?" I repeated. Joe and Jones both shot me questioning looks. "From Bayport? Because—"

"No," Mom said. "That's the strange thing. They were from a town near Atlantic City—Margate. And they said you and Joe are wanted for questioning."

"Wanted for questioning?" I repeated. Joe's brow crinkled, and Jones shook her head as if to say, *What?*

"That's right," Mom said. "I just . . . Is this about that girl who . . . ?"

"Yes," I said, "it probably is. But we spoke to them yesterday. I'm not sure why they'd need us back."

Mom cleared her throat. "It does seem strange," she said.

"Well, there's one easy way to find out," I said, looking at Joe. "We're not far from Margate now. And as it happens, we have some new information to share with the police."

Joe nodded eagerly, but on the other side of the line, Mom

sounded distinctly less enthused. "Frank, your father is getting in the car now," she said. "Why don't you wait, and he can meet you there? He can—you know—*smooth over . . .*"

Dad is a former police detective. It was true, he'd certainly "smoothed over" some misunderstandings with the police for us before. But this time, we already knew the detectives we'd be speaking with. And it seemed pretty clear we were all on the same side.

"No, don't worry, Mom," I said. "Tell Dad to stay put and not miss dinner. We'll be fine. We've spoken to these guys before. I'll call if we need anything, okay? And I'll text when we're leaving Margate. Bye!"

"But Fr—"

I hung up before my mom could protest.

I wanted to hear what the Margate police were thinking—and tell them what we'd learned—as soon as possible.

Even though we'd been there just the day before, the receptionist at the Margate police station was not exactly welcoming.

"The *Hardy* boys?" she repeated, squinting at Joe and me like we might be trying to pull a fast one on her. "And you've just walked in to see Detectives Gomez and McGill?"

"That's right," Joe said, smiling what I call his Very Good Boy Smile. It's this obsequious expression he uses to win over adults—which works, like, *way* too often. "We were here yesterday, remember? Can you tell them we're here?"

The receptionist, to her credit, did not respond to Joe's Very Good Boy Smile at all. "And who is this?" she asked, frowning at Jones, who stood behind us.

"I'm nobody," said Jones. "I mean, I'm Jones, but I don't have to talk to the detectives. I can wait out here."

The receptionist squinted even harder at Joe, then at me. "I can't tell them you're here," she said, "because they're not in the station currently. But have a seat. They're on their way back."

We nodded and settled onto a couple of hard plastic chairs. We began leafing through the years-old magazine selection and playing with our phones. But we'd still run out of ways to entertain ourselves by the time Detectives Gomez and McGill walked through the door forty minutes later.

"Speak of the devil," Gomez said, taking us in. There was not a hint of a smile on her face. Her eyes were not warm.

Even McGill, who'd been the nicer one the day before, looked mildly disgusted by us. "Let's get these boys into an interrogation room right away," he said.

The three of us had briefly discussed asking the detectives whether Jones could join us, but both of them looked so grim, none of us wanted to bring it up. Jones shook her head and waved us on, indicating that she'd wait in the lobby.

We were led into the interrogation room where Matt had been held before. I wondered suddenly where Matt was. Had he been let go?

"Take a seat," said McGill, indicating two uncomfortable-looking plastic chairs facing a square card table. He sat down on a slightly comfier-looking chair facing us.

"Excuse me for just a moment," Gomez said, softening her glare a tiny bit. "I'm going to turn on the video camera. We'll be filming this."

Filming this? I looked at Joe with alarm. We'd been in enough interrogation rooms in enough police stations to know that *filming this* is not something you want the detectives to be doing.

"Are we . . . ?" Joe began, looking from me to the detectives with a confused expression.

"Just sit," McGill instructed, pointing at the chair.

We were already sitting, but I was beginning to regret walking in here so readily.

"Ummm . . . ," I said, for lack of anything else to say.

Gomez returned, holding a manila folder, a laptop, and a flash drive. She closed the door behind her, then sat down in the chair beside McGill.

"Well," said McGill.

"Well," said Gomez.

"Ah," said Joe, looking at me awkwardly. "Okay. Well. Um. We . . ."

"We wanted to come in," I said, taking over, "because we . . . well, we have some new information."

I looked at the detectives, expecting some change in their expression—some warming, maybe even an encouraging smile. But there was no change. They looked as cold as they had since they'd walked in the front door.

"That's interesting," McGill said. "We also have some new information, which is why we drove to your home in Bayport and spoke with your mother."

I glanced at Joe. *Ahhh.* I'm not sure why I hadn't put together that the detectives would have gone to Bayport themselves. But why? Wouldn't it have been easier to farm it out to the Bayport PD? Or just call us? Maybe I should have asked Mom a few more questions before hanging up. . . .

McGill was still looking at us expectantly. "Who'd like to go first?" he asked, but his chilly expression implied that he was not terribly curious about what we were going to say.

"I would," I said quickly. I think some part of me was hoping that once the detectives knew what we knew, they would remember that we weren't the enemy. "Joe and I spoke to an online friend of Harper's today . . . and we've found what we think are some potential suspects. . . ." As briefly as I could, I explained how we'd found Von's card, spoken to him, and found out that Harper had been lying to a whole array of InkWorld posters . . . for a sum total of thousands of dollars. As I spoke, I became more and more enthusiastic, hoping that the detectives would respond in kind. *This is big!* I hoped I was saying. *We have maybe solved this case for you and maybe you could smile!*

But there was no smile. Actually, I thought I caught Detective Gomez scowling, but then she scratched her nose, so maybe she was just itchy. They glanced at each other, but their expressions did not seem to be saying, *Wow, these boys are very smart and useful.* In fact, it didn't seem like they were having any sort of positive reaction.

At all.

Which seemed super weird.

When I'd finished the whole story, there was silence. I looked at Joe, whose freaked-out expression seemed to say, *This isn't good.*

It was not.

"Well," said McGill after a few seconds. "What an interesting discovery."

Gomez let his words hang in the air for a little while before adding, "We also had an interesting discovery today. Would you like to hear about it?"

I'm guessing no? I thought, exchanging a concerned look with my brother. But it didn't seem like a good idea to voice that thought.

"Let me show you something," Gomez went on, placing the laptop on the table and waking it up. She plugged the flash drive into a USB port, pulled the whole thing over to her, and clicked around a bit. "Here," she said, turning the laptop around so we could see it.

It was security camera footage of Harper's UrMotel, but . . .

"Where is that from?" I asked, trying to place the angle. We already knew the security footage from the building itself was worthless. . . .

"It's from the apartment building next door," McGill said. "It's zoomed in significantly, which is why it's a little grainy."

It was actually super grainy. This also happened at night, making it even harder to see what was going on. But still, the footage clearly showed two figures—about Joe's and my size, and wearing baggy clothes and ski masks—either leading or dragging a third figure, with a pillowcase over her head, out onto the walkway.

"That's Harper," Joe whispered, his voice tight with concern.

"That's right," McGill replied.

"Oh God," Joe murmured.

The figures led Harper down the stairs. Then they crossed the patio, stepped onto the beach, and ran across the sand and out of the frame to the right.

"Did she go willingly?" I asked, trying to figure it all out. "I mean . . . I know her face was covered, but it didn't look like they were forcing her."

"Look again," Gomez replied, pulling the laptop closer to rewind the footage. When she turned the computer back around, she pointed to one of the figures in the ski masks, who kept gesturing to something in his pocket. "He may be threatening her with a gun right there. We can't be sure, because there's no audio. But that, combined with the pillowcase on her head, certainly seems to imply she didn't go willingly."

I stared at the laptop. The figures were so blurry, it was hard to read anything—their intention, Harper's state of mind, where they were headed.

But this was definitely enough to raise concerns.

And from the way the detectives were looking at us, I could tell where they were focusing their concerns.

"Um . . . what do you think you're seeing here?" I asked.

McGill did scowl then. "You tell me," he said.

"Uhhh . . . ," I said, not sure what to say.

He jabbed a finger at one ski-masked figure. "Like, look at his body type," he suggested. "This would appear to be a tall, young, lanky male—much like yourselves," he added.

I looked at Joe. *Uh-oh.*

"You know who he definitely *doesn't* look like," Gomez said, "is Matthew Driscoll."

"No," McGill agreed, "Mr. Driscoll is much shorter and stockier."

"*And*," Gomez added, "he has an airtight alibi."

"He does?" Joe asked, his voice a little squeaky, which was unfortunate.

"Yup," McGill replied. "He works nights at a warehouse, which happens to have time cards. He was there all night, with coworkers to vouch for him."

I caught Joe's eye again. *Not good, not good.* Were we seriously suspects here? I replayed the last few hours. The detectives coming to our house, us charging into the station like we were all old buddies. Suddenly I felt very foolish.

Then McGill leaned across the table and looked into my eyes, then Joe's. "Let me level with you," he said, his voice suddenly low and deadly serious. "We know you boys were in the apartment that night. You had plenty of time to case the joint—make note of how to break in, even how to obscure the security cameras."

Obscure the security cameras. Of course. They were operational—they were just blocked by a plant. That's something the culprit could have done—or made sure was done.

Gomez cleared her throat. "That would also explain why you had Harper's phone," she told us.

Gulp. All at once, I realized how suspicious that looked. We had a good reason—but what's the likelihood that someone would willingly give you her phone?

McGill pointed to the frozen time stamp in the corner. "So tell me, where were you boys at twelve fourteen a.m. the night Harper Anderson disappeared?"

"Officer McGill, we were home at that time," I said, "I swear."

McGill shook his head. "You know, I'm having a hard time believing that."

"And why would we hurt her?" Joe asked, leveling his gaze at McGill. He seemed to have his squeaky voice issue under control now and had morphed into what I call Cool Joe Under Fire, i.e., the guy who had saved our bacon in tense situations before.

"You tell us," McGill replied, meeting Joe's gaze without

flinching. When neither one of us spoke, he continued, "Only you boys know the truth, but we have theories. Maybe one of you had a crush on Harper, but she didn't feel the same way. So things got out of hand. You came back to confront her, and things got violent. *Something* happened, and you removed Harper from the scene."

"That *something* is the part only you boys know," Gomez added.

McGill nodded. "Then you returned to the scene of the crime in the morning to report it—throwing suspicion off yourselves." He looked from Joe to me, smiled coldly, and sat back in his seat, splaying his hands. "The perfect crime."

"Or so you thought," Gomez commented.

I looked at Joe like, *What now?*

"But we have alibis," Joe said smoothly, his cool expression giving away none of the panic I knew we were both feeling. "We did go home that night. We can prove it!"

"Can you, though?" asked McGill, resting his elbow on the arm of his chair. "Your alibis come from your parents and Frank's girlfriend—people invested in keeping you out of jail."

I felt my jaw drop. "You're saying our parents lied to you about where we were?" *But that's our whole alibi.*

"We're saying your alibi looks a lot flimsier in light of this new evidence," Gomez replied.

Joe glanced at me, and I could see in that moment that

he was beginning to panic. But he didn't show that to the police. "You can't seriously think that," he said, looking first at Gomez, then McGill. "Our father—"

"Look," Gomez said sharply, suddenly rising to her feet, knocking our file off the desk. Papers scattered everywhere, but her glare didn't waver from us. "*Your* fingerprints—both of you—were found in the apartment. We have a neighbor who reported that you were in the apartment with Harper late the night before she disappeared."

Complainy Guy. "But that guy—" I began.

"*I don't want to hear it!*" Gomez shouted. "A girl is missing! Her aunt and her boyfriend are scared sick! I don't want to dither around with you boys any longer. I want you to tell me what happened to her, right now!"

"We don't know!" Joe cried, and now I could hear the panic in his voice.

"*I think you do!*" Gomez yelled.

Joe looked at me, and the desperation in his eyes matched what I was feeling. *What do we do?* We had nothing to tell them. But it was clear they weren't going to believe that.

"Listen," I said, "we're just as worried about Harper as you are. I know this looks bad, but we're telling the truth. If you just look at the list of guys we brought—"

"Why should we believe you?" McGill asked with a sneer. "You're the most likely suspects, and you reported the crime to the police, which makes me think *you* think you understand law enforcement. Why wouldn't you lie—"

As my heart rate was climbing, there was a sudden knock on the door. McGill stopped mid-rant and turned toward it.

"I'll get it," Gomez said. She walked over to the door and opened it. I couldn't see who was on the other side, but Gomez leaned her head out, talking in hushed tones with what sounded like another woman.

"As I was saying," McGill went on, "we know you think you know how to play us. But what I want you to understand is, we're *on*—"

"Ahem." Gomez closed the door and looked at McGill. "We need to stop."

McGill looked up at her, clearly disappointed. "What do you mean?"

Gomez looked from me to Joe. "The boys' father is here," she said curtly.

TRUTH AND LIES

7

JOE

LOVE MY FATHER, BUT I DON'T THINK I'VE ever been so happy to see him in my entire life as I was when he walked into Gomez's office at the Margate police station.

"Detectives," he said, nodding at McGill and Gomez. "Boys."

They'd taken us out of the little interrogation room, and now we were crammed into Detective Gomez's not-large-or-luxurious office. I noticed photos of her with two smiling kids, around preschool age, on her desk. There was also a little statue of Snoopy dressed as a police officer.

These things made me like her more, I'll admit.

McGill cleared his throat. "I understand you have some information for us," he said.

"Better than that," Dad said, pulling a flash drive out of his shirt pocket. "I have hard evidence. Evidence that I think will make clear what these boys were up to that night."

Gomez took the drive. "Let me plug this into my laptop," she said, sitting down at her desk and opening up the slim Mac she'd brought with her from the interrogation room. There were a few weird moments where she fiddled around on her computer, and we all looked at one another awkwardly.

"You made good time," Frank said to my dad, all faux-casual.

Dad looked at him, stone-faced. "I had good reason," he said simply.

"Aha," said Gomez, clicking a key and turning the laptop around to face us all. "Here we go."

The screen showed a window of footage from a security camera. In black and white, it showed our driveway, our basketball hoop, Aunt Trudy's rosebushes. A clock in the lower right-hand corner kept track of the time. We watched for about thirty seconds until Frank's car pulled into the driveway at precisely 11:08 p.m. The car was parked and the lights went out, and then Frank and I climbed out and walked toward the house.

"Huh," said McGill. He didn't sound entirely happy.

"Yes," said Dad.

McGill coughed. "Do you have the raw footage from the camera?" he asked. "We'll have to look it all over, and just make sure it wasn't doctored. . . ."

Dad nodded at the flash drive. "It's all on there," he said. "You can watch the entire night, if you like. It will show that the boys didn't leave the house until the next morning at precisely 7:12 a.m. Which means . . ."

Gomez looked at McGill. "Frank and Joe were telling the truth. They went home that night."

McGill did not look happy about this. He didn't meet Gomez's eye, and instead seemed to stare into some middle distance, his expression souring. "They could have . . . ," he began.

"Snuck out the back door?" Dad supplied. "And gotten there how—taken a bus? A train? From Bayport to Margate, in the middle of the night?" He shook his head. "Unless you know of a different New Jersey Transit system that runs twenty-four hours a day, I think they were out of luck."

McGill looked even more annoyed. "Another car?" he suggested.

Dad shrugged. "I guess," he allowed. "They could have snuck out a back door into a waiting vehicle elsewhere on the block and gotten a ride. Considering that my sons didn't know I had this security camera installed, that would show remarkable foresight on their part. And I'm sure the security camera from the apartment complex would show an unidentified car arriving." He paused, and McGill cringed. "Right?"

McGill shook his head. "What about—Uber?" he asked.

"Sure, Uber," Dad said. "The ride-sharing service. If you

subpoena their records, I'm sure they would show whether anyone was picked up around our neighborhood in Bayport and driven to Margate in the wee hours of Saturday night." He nodded at Gomez, then McGill. "When you have that evidence, we'll happily hand over the boys. Until then . . ."

McGill groaned.

Gomez stood up, nodding back at my father. "Thank you, Mr. Hardy," she said, glancing awkwardly at McGill. "I think you've made your case. And I'd like to apologize on behalf of the Margate PD for any inconvenience to your boys." She looked at Frank and me. "I'm sorry, boys. I think it's clear now that you've been pretty up-front with us. You're free to go."

Frank and I stood eagerly. "You know," I said, unable to stop myself from looking at McGill, "one of the guys on the list we brought you might be tall and lanky, like the guys in the video."

McGill glared at me, but muttered, "We'll look into it."

Frank was allowed to drive a very relieved Jones home, but Dad insisted that I ride with him. And he gave Frank pretty clear instructions to drop off Jones and immediately head home.

"Um," I said, as Dad pulled onto the highway after approximately ten minutes of sitting in silence. Ten minutes that felt like ten hours. "Thanks, Dad. You really saved us in there."

Dad glanced at me from the driver's seat. His mouth was

set in a grim line. "Your mother told you boys not to go in there alone," he said after an excruciating pause.

"I know," I said. "We just . . . we had some information we thought they would want to pounce on. We got the usernames of at least ten more suspects—members of the InkWorld online forum—that Harper owed money to. I mean, there's no way they would have found that without us."

"And I suppose you thought the police were your friends? That they'd never suspect you?"

I stared out the windshield at the passing signs. "Sort of," I admitted. "Okay, yeah, we did. It just made sense that we should work together! We're all looking for the same thing."

Dad grunted. "That's how it *should* work, yes, but you have to learn to think like a cop. They need to solve the case quickly, get the culprit off the street. They're going to look at the most obvious suspects first. Which are you two."

I didn't respond, just swallowed hard.

"*You* were in the apartment that night. *You* had her phone. *You* were there when the crime was reported. Really, Joe: Why *wouldn't* they suspect you?"

I sighed, feeling silly. "I don't know."

Dad shook his head. He was silent for a few seconds. Then he said, "Your problem, and your brother's problem, is that you think you're invincible. You've solved enough cases and come out okay, you think nothing can ever happen to you. Well, it can. It *can*, son."

He glanced over at me, and I met his gaze. He looked more upset than I was expecting.

"I know, Dad."

"*Do* you?"

I looked back out the windshield. The world was flying by at seventy miles an hour. I felt incredibly lucky to be in that car, on my way home, and not sitting in a bare cell at the Margate police station.

"I do."

We rode in silence for a few minutes.

"I didn't know you had a security camera on the driveway," I said finally, turning to look at Dad. "I didn't know you had any cameras on the house."

The corner of Dad's mouth turned up. "Yeah. Well. It really comes in handy, with you boys' odd extracurricular activities."

I chuckled.

"Weren't you supposed to be studying for the SAT today?"

Dad's voice was just casual, no judgment, but it still made me feel bad. "I tried," I said honestly. "I just couldn't concentrate. You know what it's like . . . trying to focus on anything else before a case is solved?"

Dad shook his head, but then smiled. "I do know." He paused, then added, "Listen. If I can't convince you to stop thinking about this case, can we at least agree that you and Frank will never charge into a police station for questioning again without a lawyer? Or at least your dear old dad?"

I nodded. "Yeah, Dad. We can agree to that."

We both watched the road for a while. All this talk about "the case" had reminded me that even after today's crazy adventures, Harper was still out there somewhere . . . missing.

Everyone knows that the longer someone is missing, the smaller the chance that he or she will be found alive.

I shuddered, thinking about where Harper might be, who she might be with.

I just hoped she was okay.

That night Frank, Jones, and I were are all sitting around the living room, trying (and failing) to pay attention to a movie. I'd decided to start fresh with studying in the morning.

The movie was something about aliens. Or maybe cars that turn into aliens. I couldn't really tell, because every time I managed to pay attention for more than thirty seconds, something would remind me of Harper, and I'd spend the next five minutes imagining some new terrifying scenario of what had happened to her.

"What if she was trying to ditch her phone on purpose?" I said out loud, as something exploded on the television and no one seemed to notice.

"What do you mean?" Jones asked. "I offered her mine. And she didn't coordinate with me or anything."

"I know," I said. "But maybe she . . . planned it?"

"Why?" Jones asked. Her incredulous look made me real-ize I was grasping at straws.

"I don't know," I admitted, sinking down into the couch.

Frank ran a hand through his hair and let out a sigh. "We all keep thinking about it. I feel like there's a piece of the puzzle we're missing," he said. "Why did Harper collect the money? Was she working with Matt, or trying to escape him?"

"We've all seen her messages on InkWorld," I said. "Von was right, she told a different lie to every guy she asked for money."

"Right," said Frank. "So it's impossible to know whether any of those stories are true."

Jones lifted up her phone. "You guys . . . there *is* one person who could probably clear up a lot of these questions for us—and I just happen to have his number."

Frank stared at her. "Do you mean Matt?"

Jones nodded.

I shuffled my feet. "Guys, I don't know. . . . We've already made some risky moves in this investigation." I caught Frank's eye, and he looked away. I'd caught him up on the *Dad is majorly disappointed in us* chat we'd had in the car. We'd both agreed it was time to start being more careful. "Matt could be dangerous. Maybe we should avoid getting too involved with him."

"But remember," Frank said, "the police say his alibi is airtight. And Matt seemed sincere when he said he and Harper were working things out."

"See?" said Jones. "And besides . . ." She paused, and

suddenly a look of real worry came over her face. "He may be the only one who can tell us the truth about Harper's life . . . before it's too late."

Too late. I pictured Harper trapped somewhere, desperately pounding on a locked door, waiting for us to save her. Maybe we were really her only hope. Matt was a controlling jerk, and she'd made so many enemies . . . who else would try to find her?

But then I remembered something.

"That's not true," I said, pointing at Jones. "Matt *isn't* the only one who can tell us about Harper's life."

She looked nonplussed. "Who, then?"

I turned to Frank. "Remember when we first discovered she was missing?" I asked. "We called someone. Her—"

"Aunt!" Frank's face lit with recognition. "Matt said her aunt raised her."

"That's right," I said. "And her number would be in Harper's contacts."

Jones ran over to the desktop, where we'd stored the information from Harper's phone. "I'll look for it."

Frank was looking a bit more hopeful. "Right, her aunt," he said. "I'd feel better about calling her than risking contact with Matt."

Jones was typing away on the computer. "I've got it," she said.

Frank stood up. "All right . . . let's make the call, then."

Jones turned back to the desktop to read off the number . . .

but then stopped suddenly. She paused, frowning, and then shook her head. "Some conversations are best had in person, don't you agree?"

I glanced at Frank. "Maybe?" I couldn't help remembering that Harper lived in Pennsylvania. An even longer drive from Bayport than Atlantic City or Margate.

"Just hear me out," Jones went on. "Harper's aunt has no idea who we are, or what our intentions are. I think we have to go there. Let's call and try to set up a time to meet. I think we have to talk this out."

Frank looked thoughtful. "Maybe if we're there, we can learn a little more about her life. Get a feel for it, you know? Maybe learn something no one else would have told us."

Jones beamed at him. "Exactly."

Frank looked at me, regret in his eyes. "I'm sorry, Joe," he said. "Jones and I can go alone, if you like. I know you still have to study for the—"

"Don't be silly," I interrupted him. "When it comes to this case, we're all in it together." *And there's no way I'd get anything done, anyway.*

Frank nodded. "All right, then. Let's call this woman. And tomorrow morning, we'll head for Pennsylvania."

THE TRUTH HURTS

8

FRANK

WELL, HELLO." HARPER'S AUNT PATTY opened her screen door and stepped back to let Joe, Jones, and me inside. She was short and stout, with long, straight gray hair pulled back and clipped to the top of her head, and dark eyes with thick eyelashes. She was wearing a red T-shirt with a quilt design on it and some faded blue jeans. She sounded a little nervous, but I supposed I couldn't blame her. All she knew was that we were here to talk about Harper, her missing niece. Joe thought it best not to tell her anything more. But I could imagine she'd probably spent a lot of time over the last twelve hours wondering what on earth we'd say, what we might know.

We all walked into the small cape-style cottage, Joe

stretching his back. It was his unsubtle way of saying *Thanks for sticking me in the backseat again.* But what was I supposed to do? Jones had called shotgun.

It had taken four hours to drive to Pottsville, Pennsylvania. We'd left at eight in the morning, so it was now about lunchtime. We were smack-dab in the middle of the state of Pennsylvania, in a pretty remote, small town. I was pretty sure most of Aunt Patty's neighbors were cows.

Inside, the cottage was cozy and cramped. Boxes of what looked like craft supplies lined the walls. A sewing machine was jammed into the middle of the living room, facing a small TV. "Why don't you come into the kitchen?" Patty asked, leading the way down a small hallway. "I made some sandwiches."

We all followed Patty down the hall to the rear of the cottage. We passed two closed doors off the hallway, which I guessed were bedrooms or bathrooms. The kitchen was sunny and decorated with wallpaper covered with lemons. Patty gestured to a small wooden table that had been set with four places, and a pile of sandwiches on a plate.

We all sat down and dug in gratefully. The sandwiches were egg salad, and I was so starving and tired, they tasted amazing.

"Thank you so much for this," Jones said with a smile. "It was really kind of you to have us over."

Patty didn't smile back. "Well," she said, "you wouldn't tell me anything on the phone."

True. Jones and I exchanged awkward glances.

"Ms. Haverill . . . ," I began.

"Patty," she corrected me.

"Patty," I said. "Well, Jones got to know Harper online, and then we all met her at Comic-Con right before she disappeared."

Patty gave a tense nod.

"We've been trying to figure out where she might have gone," Jones added.

Patty narrowed her eyes at Jones. "Are you working with the police? Because I've already talked to them."

"No, we're just friends of Harper's," Joe explained. "*Concerned* friends. We wondered if you could tell us anything about her life, anything that might help us figure out where she is?"

Patty let out an unimpressed-sounding grunt. "If you all are her friends," she said, "then you probably know more than me. Even when she lived here, half the time Harper treated me like a landlord."

Jones took a sip of iced tea and swallowed. "How did you come to be Harper's guardian?"

Patty sighed. "Well. Sure. Let's get into it." She pushed a wisp of hair behind her ear. "I took Harper in when my sister, Harper's mother, died."

"That's sad," said Jones. "I mean, for you and for Harper. How old was she?"

"She was eight," Patty said. "Really sad. But I love Harper like my own daughter. Always have."

Jones nodded slowly. "And Harper's father?"

Patty scowled. "Her father was never in the picture. A rolling stone, that one. That's where Harper gets it."

Jones glanced at me, then Joe. "Sorry? Where Harper gets what?"

Patty shook her head, staring into her lap, then looked up at us. She looked into my eyes, then Joe's, then Jones's. "Look," she said, "it's nice of you kids to worry so much about my niece. And it's terrible that Harper has gone missing, but that girl has always been . . . restless."

Restless. I thought of the online messages, the money. *Did Harper just want to get out of this town?*

"What do you mean, restless?" Joe asked.

Patty fixed an unimpressed gaze on him. "I mean *restless* by restless. You know what it means. She ran with the wrong crowd, got into trouble, dropped out of school. She was always talking about going to the city and going to art school, but that girl couldn't keep a job long enough to save up any money. She'd get fired, and it was always someone else's fault. They gave her the wrong schedule. Or her boss didn't like her. Or someone sabotaged the fryer machine." She shook her head again. "Ridiculous stuff. I love her, but she's work."

I looked at Joe. "Matt told us that they were saving up for a down payment on a house," I said to Patty.

Patty frowned at me. "Well, I don't know anything about that. I can see Matt wanting that, but Harper? She's still too . . ."

"Too?" Jones prompted, and took a bite of her sandwich.

Patty looked at her. "Wild," she said, jutting out her chin a little. We were all silent for a few seconds—silent enough that we could hear a car drive past. *So someone else does live around here,* I thought.

Then she scowled. "Listen, like I said, you all are very nice to worry about my niece. But honestly? Whatever the police might believe, I don't think anyone 'took' Harper anywhere."

Joe raised an eyebrow. "What do you think happened to her, then?"

Patty shrugged. "You know what? Harper tried to run away five different times before she was sixteen. I half think she got messed up with some of those same kids she hung with when she was a teenager, and took off with them."

I put down my sandwich. As good as it was, I'd been too engrossed in this conversation to take a bite for the last few minutes, anyway.

"Um," said Jones, looking a little flustered by this new theory. "Why? I mean, who were these kids?"

Patty snorted. "*Bad* kids," she said, "that's all you have to know. Always up to something they shouldn't be."

"Like what?" Joe asked frankly.

"Stealing, running away, all of it." Patty stared at the table for a minute, then looked up at us. "See, I've been getting threatening messages. Messages from people trying to find Harper. I think she got messed up with these kids again, and then panicked. Did something. Maybe *took* something. And now they want it back."

Joe wiped his mouth with a napkin and stood up. "You've been getting threatening messages?" he asked. "Did you save any? Could we hear them?"

Patty looked from Joe, to me, to Jones, her expression never changing from "unimpressed." Still, she shrugged and stood. "I suppose."

She walked over to the counter, which I now saw held a denim purse. She rooted around in it for a few seconds and then pulled out a smartphone clad in a quilt-patterned case. After tapping on the phone for a few seconds, she walked back to the table and held it out so we could hear.

"Hey." The voice on the first message was low, raspy, and breathy. "I know you know where Harper is. Tell her I'm not forgetting. And if she won't make it right, I'm coming after you."

I looked at Jones and Joe. *Is it someone she lied to online?*

"Patty Haverill," the next message began. This guy was growling—clearly trying to disguise his voice. "Harper owes me. She knows it. If I can't find her . . ." The growl rose into a freaky cackle, the kind of thing you'd expect to hear in a haunted house. Then the message abruptly ended.

"Th-that's, um, that's really," Jones stammered. "That's really . . . concerning."

"Hello," the next message began. This was a woman, surprisingly, with a slight British accent. "Patty Haverill, I'm calling for your niece, Harper, from Juniper Credit Solutions. As I've said on my previous messages, we're collecting for American Express, with whom Harper opened a credit account with a five-thousand-dollar limit and took a twenty-five-hundred-dollar cash loan on it, which she never paid back. Ms. Haverill, while Harper is no longer a minor, so you're not *legally* responsible for Harper's debts, we *are* legally authorized to continue calling until—"

Patty tapped the button to hang up. "You get the idea," she said.

Jones, Joe, and I all looked at one another, nodding. "The thing is," Joe said, "we also recently learned that Harper owed money to several people. Like, even more people than have left you messages."

Patty suddenly turned tense. She glared at Joe. "I have nothing to do with that girl's debts," she said. "You heard the lady on the phone: I'm not responsible. You can't threaten me!"

"Wait, wait," I said, patting the air in a *calm down* gesture. "Joe didn't mean . . . Harper never stole money from *us*."

"We were just trying to figure out what it was for," Jones added, "especially if people were trying to get it back. . . . It might give us a clue as to where she is!"

But Patty wasn't listening. She'd already moved away from us and was backed against the counter, looking panicked. I watched as her hand fumbled behind her toward a large block of knives. "You get out of my house," she said. "Now I know what kind of people you are. . . ."

"We're totally normal people!" Joe shouted, clearly getting frustrated. "Look, we're all on the same side, aren't we? Don't we all want to find Harper?"

Patty's hand found a small paring knife, which she jabbed in front of her. "I just want peace and quiet!" she yelled. "Time to work on my *quilts*!"

Joe groaned. I could tell he was getting worked up, which was not good. "Isn't your niece more impor—"

But Joe never got to finish his sentence. Because at that moment, the front door banged open, and a vaguely familiar voice yelled from the living room. "Patty?!"

"In here!" she screamed, pointing the knife at us with every muscle in her body.

We heard a large person come stomping down the short hallway.

And then Matt was standing in the kitchen door—pointing a hunting rifle at the three of us.

"OMIGOD!" yelled Jones, shaking.

But Matt didn't even seem to notice Jones. He came barging toward me and Joe, leading with the rifle.

"Wait!" I cried. "Matt, we—"

But Matt did not want to talk. This soon became

incredibly clear, as he got closer and his finger reached for the trigger.

"OUT OF THE HOUSE!" he screamed. "NOW!!!!!"

We didn't hesitate. I looked behind me and noticed a back door in the kitchen, leading into the wooded backyard. I ran to it, opened it up, and ran out.

Joe followed me down the few steps to the woods, then Jones.

"We'll go now," I said, turning back to the house. "We'll get in our car and—"

But once again, Matt didn't seem interested in listening.

Because he was running out the back door after us—with us still in the rifle's sights.

"If you want to live," he growled, "I'd start running!"

I stared into the dark, gnarled woods. I looked at Joe and Jones.

We ran.

SURVIVAL 9

JOE

WHEN A CRAZY GUNMAN IS CHASING you, your brother, and your brother's girlfriend who you've recently decided isn't that bad through the woods in Pennsylvania, you have to think quickly. I decided to try to anger said gunman to get him to split off and follow me, giving Frank and Jones a chance to escape.

I know, I know. I'm very brave. Not to brag or anything.

So I screamed at Matt. "Hey, man! We know you did it! We know your crazy butt kidnapped Harper because that's how *crazy* you are!"

It worked. The rifle turned in my direction, and I cut to the right, past a dangerously leaning shed and into a copse of scraggly pine trees.

Matt followed.

Again, I don't mean to brag, but I run cross-country. I'm kind of made for it, with the long legs and agility and whatnot. Plus, this is my life, you know? If anyone thinks this was the first time I'd tried to outrun a guy with a rifle who was trying to kill me, well, I've got some stories to share.

So I just concentrated on running, and I ran. Through trees and over piles of leaves, I ran. Around thick brush and smack-dab into a pile of what might have been deer poop, I ran.

I could hear Matt panting behind me. He was crazy and he had a rifle, but he had *not* run cross-country. I could tell.

After about ten minutes I came to a clearing with a huge, squarish boulder in the middle of it. I ran to the boulder and crouched down on the other side. When I heard Matt lumbering toward me, I scooted around to the other side of the boulder, trying to keep him exactly opposite me.

When he got to the side where I should have been, I could hear Matt curse.

"Dude," I yelled from the other side of the boulder. "You don't have to kill us, you know. We'll leave quietly. Don't we all want the same thing?"

He ran around the boulder, his heavy footsteps crunching in the dried grass. I scooted back to the original side.

"Come on, dude," he groaned, panting, when he realized I wasn't there, either. He stopped for a minute, seeming to try to catch his breath, and then spoke again. "What do you mean, we want the same thing?"

I opened my mouth to answer, but then stopped.

Something interesting had appeared on the edge of my vision, where the clearing turned back into woods. Something bright red.

Jones's lipstick.

I turned to look. Jones and Frank were there! Jones held up something, but I couldn't tell what it was—it was mostly hidden by her fist. I shook my head, just a tiny movement. *I'm cool. Stay where you are.*

"We want Harper brought home safe," I said to Matt. "Don't we?"

I heard Matt pant a few more times. Apparently, he hadn't caught his breath yet. "You know, honestly, I almost don't care what happens to her at this point," he said. "I want her to be okay, but . . . she *left* me. And she left a hell of a mess behind her."

"You know about the money," I said. "What she owed."

"I do now. The police kindly filled me in." Matt gave what sounded like a bitter laugh.

"Was that for the two of you?" I asked. "For the house?"

"No," Matt replied sharply. "It's not anything I knew about. She just left me to deal with the fallout."

"You and Patty," I said, after a moment.

"Yeah," Matt said. "That's why Patty called me here. She thought maybe you were some of the people Harper owed money to, coming to try to shake her down, or whatever. But she wasn't sure, and she wanted to hear what you had to say. So she asked me to come be her bodyguard, but I was late." He sighed. "Work."

Now that Matt seemed calmer, I decided to take a chance. To plead my case. "Man, please believe me when I—"

But I was interrupted by some kind of war cry.

"AAAAAAAAHHHHHHHHHH!"

Out of the corner of my eye, I saw Jones come flying from the woods, a small cylinder clutched in front of her, aiming straight for Matt's side of the boulder. I heard Matt shift, and then heard Jones's scream increase in volume . . . and then I heard a loud "SHHHHHH!!!" sound.

Then Matt screamed. "WHAT THE . . . ?!"

And there was a clatter as something—and maybe *someone*—fell to the ground.

I jumped up from my crouch and ran around the boulder. Frank was running from the woods too. I realized he must have run after Jones, but my attention had been too focused on her to notice.

Matt was lying on the ground on the other side of the boulder, his face bright red, eyes closed and swelling quickly. Jones was holding out a small spray can.

"What is that?" I asked.

Jones looked up at me, as casual as if I'd asked what the weather was going to be. "Pepper spray," she said. "I couldn't let him *kill* you, Joe."

THE LETTER

10

FRANK

I KNEW JONES WAS A KEEPER, BUT EVEN *I* WAS impressed that she'd risked her life to pepper-spray Matt and save Joe.

I mean, of course she would have done it for me. But *Joe*.

An hour or so after the heroic rescue, we were all sitting comfortably Patty's living room again. Matt (who, in a surprising twist, had vouched for us with Patty) was holding a washcloth soaked with milk to his eyes. Milk was the antidote for pepper spray—Jones googled it. And it seemed to be working, sort of.

"I never want to be pepper-sprayed again," Matt moaned.

"Maybe you should never chase someone with a hunting rifle again," said Jones unapologetically. "Just some advice."

"So you really just came here for answers about Harper,"

Patty said, looking somewhat disbelievingly at the collection of people in her living room.

"That's right," I said. "We're trying to find her. We really want to make sure she's okay."

"Why?" Patty asked, frowning. "You barely know her."

"It's what we do," Joe said, shrugging. "We kind of . . . figure things out."

Matt sighed, pulling the washcloth away from his face, which was still pretty red. "I'm sorry I chased you," he said. "I guess I was just kind of amped up after getting *this*."

He reached into his jeans pocket and pulled out a folded piece of paper. I stood up and walked over to him, and he handed it to me.

I sat back down between Joe and Jones on the coach and unfolded it. Joe and Jones drew closer to read it with me. It was a letter, printed out from a computer.

You know what happened. We know everything. The debt will be repaid, one way or another. Pay me now, immediately, or deal with the consequences.

"This doesn't mean they have Harper, but it could mean they know things are pretty bad. . . . I mean, they know where she lives."

"Yeah, it sounds like a threat," Jones filled in.

I turned to Matt. "How did you get this?"

He reached into his other pocket and pulled out an

envelope. "It was in my mailbox this morning, in this," he said, handing the envelope to me. It was blank, with no postmark.

"Hand-delivered," Joe said.

"Apparently," Matt agreed.

I looked at Joe and Jones, frowning. "Did you take this to the police?" I asked Matt.

"Uh, *no*," he scoffed. "Those guys and me aren't exactly friends."

I remembered what Gomez had said after we'd first been interviewed and we'd passed Matt in the other interrogation room: *Mr. Driscoll isn't going home any time soon.* It had sure sounded as if they liked him as the main suspect—until he turned out to have an airtight alibi. He probably didn't want to call attention to himself.

"This letter writer sounds like one of the online victims," Joe muttered, "but which one could it be?"

Jones shrugged. "Don't forget," she said, "we just found out Harper owed money to a credit card company too. Who knows who else she might owe money to? Maybe it's someone we don't even know about yet."

I looked at Matt, who looked miserable, probably for a lot of reasons. "You really don't know what she wanted the money for?" I asked. "You're sure it wasn't a down payment?"

Matt groaned and shook his head. "For the last time," he said, "I don't know why she took that money. I didn't even know about it until after she disappeared. She was so—I don't know—" He fluttered his hand like a bird desperate to get out of a cage.

"Restless?" Patty supplied.

Matt nodded. "That's it. Restless." He sighed. "I loved her, man. I wanted so badly to settle down with her. But she never seemed ready."

"It sounds like you *fought* about it," Jones pointed out, her mouth twisted into a skeptical scowl. "Like you tried to force the issue, control her. Some of the texts you sent while we had her phone were *scary*."

Matt blinked, then nodded again. "Yeah," he said, a little sadly. "I thought I could change her, you know? Like if I was serious enough about it, if I was mean enough, I could make her more ready."

"That's really messed up," I said.

Matt swallowed hard, closing his eyes. "Yeah. I can see that better now. It got ugly once or twice. I never hurt her, but I scared her, and that really is messed up."

Jones glared at him. "*Yeah,*" she said pointedly.

Matt opened his eyes. "I know. I do. I'm trying to work on my temper, but maybe that's not enough."

"I think you should talk to someone," Joe suggested, "before you do more than scare somebody."

"You're right," Matt said after a pause. "Anyway, the only thing I can think of is, she liked to talk about moving to a big city, going to art school. Maybe that's what she collected the money for?"

I looked at Joe and Jones. *Moving to a city? Art school?* It seemed like as good a lead as any . . . and also our only lead, so there was that.

"Can we take the letter to the Margate police?" I asked Matt. "Or we could give you a ride, if you want to come along."

Patty snorted. "You would take him in your car with you after he chased you with a rifle?"

"Well," Jones said, "I'd still have my pepper spray."

I waved the letter. "We've been honest with you all along, Patty. *All* we want is to figure out what happened to Harper."

Patty looked from me to Joe to Jones, then shook her head. "You all are some good friends."

Matt stood up. "You take it," he said. "I'm eager to know what happens, and that Harper is safe. But I think I should stay here. No matter what's happened to her . . . I realize now I need to let her go." He pushed the washcloth back onto his eyes. "And start working on myself."

CRIMES OF PASSION

11

JOE

MATT COULD HAVE WRITTEN THE LETTER, you know." It occurred to me just as we pulled off the highway in Margate, after swinging by Bayport to drop off Jones in time for her evening shift at the coffee shop. Matt and I had been through a lot together that afternoon—he tried to kill me, we helped him through a nasty pepper spray attack—and that had a tendency to create a bond. But Matt was still the suspect with the most obvious motivation for hurting Harper: jealousy.

We couldn't lose sight of that.

"It was printed out, no postmark," I went on. "Matt could have written it to throw suspicion off himself. He said the police had told him Harper owed people money."

Frank frowned, staring out the windshield. "But why?" he asked. "The police already cleared him, because he was at work. He didn't need to do anything to throw their suspicion off him."

I shrugged. "His alibi doesn't mean he couldn't have hired people to abduct Harper. Maybe he knew there was more evidence out there. Maybe—" A horrible thought occurred to me, and I broke off before I finished that sentence.

"What?" Frank prompted.

"Well," I said carefully, "Harper hasn't been heard from since she vanished. Maybe, somewhere, there's a . . ."

Frank swallowed loudly as he seemed to get it. "Let's not talk about that," he said. "Let's . . . take this to the police, and they can at least check it for fingerprints and DNA."

I nodded, trying to push the horrible thought away and just focus on this lead. "Right. That would give them a hint as to who wrote it."

Gomez and McGill weren't *thrilled* to see us—especially McGill—but when we showed them that we'd brought new evidence, they seemed to warm up.

"You're still working this case?" Gomez asked, as we settled into her office. She sounded a teeny bit impressed.

"We care about Harper," I said. "We just want to find out what happened to her."

Gomez breathed out through her nostrils, handing the letter over to McGill. He took it, still looking like he'd swallowed a lemon. But as he started to read, his expression softened.

"We've been looking into the online victims, actually," Gomez explained, "but most of them have alibis—and many of them live hundreds or even thousands of miles away. Honestly, we're running out of potential suspects."

"What about Matt?" I asked, remembering my realization in the car. "He had an alibi, I know—but couldn't he have hired someone to take Harper? To abduct her, or . . . whatever?" I didn't want to think about the specifics of what "whatever" could mean.

Gomez shook her head. "We don't think—"

But to my surprise, McGill interrupted. "It's not the worst theory," he said, looking thoughtful. "Of all the suspects, Matt definitely has the clearest motive." He paused, looking off into space. But then he let out a disappointed sound. "Although crimes of passion are usually, well, passionate. It would be very unusual for the abductor to hire someone hundreds of miles away."

"But not impossible," Gomez added. "We'll look into it."

McGill passed the letter back to Gomez. "We'll also test this for fingerprints and DNA," he said. "See what we find. If that's it, boys . . ."

I was suddenly thinking about the last time we were in this office: when Dad had shown the security footage from our house. And McGill had come out with his crazy theory about us taking an Uber, and Dad had said . . .

"One more thing," I said suddenly. "We know you checked

the security footage from the lobby and the walkway near the apartment, but did you ever look at the footage from the UrMotel parking lot? Or anywhere else, like any hallways?"

Gomez looked surprised by my question, but McGill looked annoyed, and maybe a little embarrassed. "We didn't find any evidence that you boys had gotten into another car or taken an Yber," he said, adding bitterly. "Another point to the Hardy boys."

I shook my head. "Yeah, cool, but I'm not worried about that. I'm just wondering if you saw anything else of interest."

Gomez and McGill exchanged a look. "No," Gomez said finally. "We did watch the footage, but those cameras showed normal activity—people Geraldine identified as guests. Nothing helpful."

"Could we see all the footage?" I asked hopefully.

McGill raised his eyebrows but shrugged. Gomez tilted her head. "Okay," she said. "I mean, I don't see why not."

After McGill headed back to his office, and Gomez took off to find the footage, Frank leaned over to me. "What are you up to?" he asked. "We're already going to be late getting home. What do you think we're going to find in this haystack?"

"A needle, I'm hoping," I said. "Specifically, I'm wondering if there's any chance Matt showed up that night."

WE'LL BE HOME LATE TONIGHT, I texted Mom a couple of hours later. Frank and I were still in the police station and had already sifted through hours of security footage.

Gomez and McGill were right about one thing: it wasn't super-thrilling stuff. In fact, it mostly showed guests moving around. I'd already recognized Complainy Guy (as Frank called him) walking down to the lobby a few times, but there was nothing you might call "unusual." We'd already watched ourselves arrive and leave.

"What time is it?" Frank asked, yawning.

"In real life or in the footage?" I asked.

"Both."

I pulled out my phone and lit it up. "It's eight thirteen p.m. for real-time Joe and Frank." Then I put my phone away and gestured to the numbers on the lower right corner of the screen. "In UrMotel time, it's two forty-five a.m."

Frank grunted. Things had gotten real quiet in the UrMotel footage. Every so often someone would come downstairs to have a smoke on the patio, or to get a drink or ice from the machine. But otherwise, it was kind of . . . boring. It was making my eyelids heavy. The pizza Gomez and McGill had let us order about an hour before lay nearly demolished on a table nearby. I felt a pizza coma coming on. . . . *Should have ordered a Mountain Dew too . . .*

"Who's that?" Frank suddenly asked, making me jump a few inches in my seat. After blinking a few times to focus, I realized he was pointing to a someone with a baseball cap pulled low over his eyes who was crossing the lobby.

"Look," Frank whispered as the figure walked across the lobby.

I looked, and my jaw dropped.

The figure was wearing Chucks. Specifically, Von's rather unique Batman-symbol Converse sneakers.

I looked at my brother, as he put my thoughts into words. "Seriously?" Frank wondered out loud. *"Him?"*

BATMAN RETURNS

12

FRANK

CAN'T BELIEVE YOU ORDERED THAT."

"Whuuut?" Joe looked up, chastened, but the effect was kind of ruined by the fact that his face was jammed full of Cowboy Burger. A Cowboy Burger—at least at the Supreme Diner—is a cheeseburger with a fried egg on top, covered in baked beans and, yeah, still served on a bun.

It was gross, and nearly impossible to eat. Nobody would order this except Joe. It was even on the last page of the menu, the one no sane person ever gets to.

I shook my head. "We're on a *case*," I hissed at him. The Margate police had agreed that it made sense for us to talk to Von first, since we had spoken to him earlier, and see if we could get at the truth. If Von admitted to anything, they were waiting in a patrol car outside and were prepared to arrest him in the parking lot. "You're wearing a wire, remember? We're here to get the guy who took Harper—once and for all! Do you really want to gross out Gomez and McGill with every chew and swallow and burp?"

Joe looked wounded. "I'm *hungry*," he said.

"You had three slices of pizza!"

"Five is my norm! I was distracted by the footage!"

I shoved Joe in the shoulder. "Finish that thing."

Joe shoved what remained of the Cowboy Burger into his mouth and began devouring it.

Von walked in the front door of the diner and spotted us right away. It was pretty quiet at ten p.m. on a weeknight. He walked over to us eagerly, his eyes bright.

"So what do you think?" he started when he was still a good ten feet away. "Does she still have it? Is there any chance of getting it back? Or did she buy something with it, and I could try to get that. . . ."

We'd texted Von, claiming that we'd been digging into the Harper situation and had a fairly good idea of what she might have done with his money. It was a lie, of course, but an effective one, because here he was.

"Actually," I said, gesturing to the seat across from us, "you might want to sit down, Von. This is going to be a deep conversation."

Von looked confused, but he sat. "Deep?" he asked. Then his eyes widened. "Oh, man, was Harper into some weird stuff? Was my money used for something illegal? Am *I* in trouble?"

Joe burped, which cut the tension considerably. "Excuse me," he said.

Von shook his head. "It's cool, man."

I took the pause in conversation as an opportunity to pull a printout from my pocket. "Von," I said, unfolding it, "I want you to look at this."

Von looked at the black-and-white image and his face paled.

"Note the date and time stamp," Joe said, wiping his face with his napkin.

Von looked up at Joe, clearly trying to look confused, but looking more like a freaked-out squirrel. "Ah . . . where is this place?"

Joe winced. "Oh, come on," he said. "You know this already . . . but this is at the building where Harper's UrMotel apartment was located."

Von looked from the picture to me, back to the picture, and then down at his lap.

"You were there," I pointed out. "We asked you all about what you knew about Harper. You never said—"

Von sighed and then took a quick breath. "Okay, but I can—I can—"

"You can what?" I prompted. "How about this? You can tell us what really happened that night."

"Yeah," Joe added. "No more of this *I wouldn't hurt a fly* crap. You clearly know a lot more than you let on."

Von looked at Joe, then turned away, looking around the diner. "I don't, though," he said in a helpless voice.

I slammed my hand down on the edge of the printout. "Are you serious?" I asked.

Von looked back at me nervously, then said, "Okay, okay, I see how this looks. I get it. That's why I didn't tell you guys before that I went to her UrMotel—I knew it would look bad."

"It does," Joe said. "It looks *very bad*."

"But I was desperate," said Von.

I glanced at Joe. "Desperate" is a common description of how people were feeling before they committed a crime. "Desperate" does not lead to good outcomes.

Von spread his hands, appealing to us. "Harper stole my whole new car fund!" he said. "Do you know how long it took me to save up that money? Do you know what being a comics dealer pays? *Not much!*"

Joe scowled, unimpressed. "How about we stick to what you did that night?" he asked.

"Yeah," I agreed, nodding. "We can get to the whys and hows later."

Von sat up straighter. "Okay. Okay. So I found you guys at the convention, which you know, but after I talked to you . . . I hid." His face was flushing. "I followed you. I saw you meet back up with Harper, and I followed you to her UrMotel."

Joe was listening, rapt, eyebrows raised.

Von paused and took a breath, looking down at the table. "I waited until you guys left with Jones."

As much as I'd thought I was prepared for this conversation, my stomach twisted. Joe didn't look like his Cowboy Burger was resting comfortably either.

"And what . . . you were angrier than you thought?" my brother prompted, looking horrified. "You confronted Harper, and things got out of control?"

Von shook his head emphatically. "No, no," he insisted. "That's the thing—I never even saw Harper!"

"You never saw her?" I repeated, confused. "Why, because you had someone abduct her for you? Why were you even there?"

Von sighed and placed his hands on the table. "No, I was going to see Harper," he said. "I wasn't planning to hurt her—I just wanted to ask her about the money. Tell her how much it had meant to me, see if she would agree to pay me back." He paused and looked out the window. "But I never even got past the patio! I went up the stairs that seemed to lead to her room, but I got stopped a few steps up by a guy who demanded to know what I was doing there."

"A guy?" I asked. "What did he look like?" But I already had an idea, and I could tell from Joe's face that he did too.

Von looked thoughtful. "Big guy, shaved head," he said. "Kind of . . . thick eyebrows?"

"How old?" Joe asked.

"I dunno, early thirties, maybe? Definitely an adult, not like, a college kid or whatever."

Complainy Guy. The guy who'd threatened to call the cops on us when we were talking in Harper's room. I could tell that Joe was thinking the same thing. Was Complainy Guy just enough of a busybody that he prowled the halls, acting like an unpaid security guard? And if so—how *had* someone gotten to Harper? Was Complainy Guy involved? Had he looked the other way, for a price?

"I thought you were desperate," Joe said. "This was your car fund, remember?"

"Yeah," said Von, looking like he didn't understand the question.

I jumped in. "I think what Joe means is, is that all it took to scare you off—a threat from some random guy?"

But Von shook his head. "Oh, no. It was *not* just a threat. You didn't let me finish."

He stopped, and Joe and I stared at him.

"Okay," I said finally, annoyed. "Go head, tell us the rest."

Von nodded, satisfied. "The dude had a *gun*."

"A gun?" I asked, looking at Joe. "Complainy Guy?"

"It was super tiny," Von went on. "I wasn't even sure it was real at first. But then I figured I didn't want to stick around to find out. I took off fast!"

Joe looked at me and laughed. "Complainy Guy had a gun the whole time. I guess it's good we didn't challenge him, then!"

When Von looked confused, Joe explained, "Frank and

I ran into this guy too—he kind of broke up our party. We thought he was really annoying, but we had no idea. . . ."

I'd stopped listening to the explanation, though. My mind was whirring with another idea.

Just a tiny thing . . .

Suddenly a pair of fingers snapped in front of my face. I startled and saw Joe trying to get my attention, asking what I wanted to do. Von was staring at me too, looking equal parts confused and hopeful.

"You can go, Von," I said with certainty.

"Wait, what?" Joe asked, looking from me to Von. "Just like that? You're totally sure?"

"Yeah," I said. "I believe him—he didn't do anything to Harper. But, dude"—I looked up at Von, who was getting nervously to his feet—"stop giving money to strangers on the Internet."

He nodded. Then, a few seconds later, he laughed, as if on a delay. "Right! Yeah, I learned my lesson! Don't worry about me! And thanks, guys—I really do hope you find her." Without another word, Von turned and scurried away, clearly not wanting to press his luck.

I spread out the printed photo with my hands and stared at it.

Von walked out the front door and it shut behind him, the bell that hung over it dinging merrily. Joe looked from the door to me.

"That's it," he mused sadly, "our last lead. God, Frank, what if we never find her?"

Our phones buzzed before I had a chance to respond. It was from Officer Gomez.

RAN LETTER FOR PRINTS. MATCHES ONE OF THE USER-NAMES, BUT HE HAS SOLID ALIBI. DON'T THINK THERE'S ANYTHING THERE. SORRY, GUYS.

Joe groaned. "Okay, now that's really it. No more leads."

I stood up, carefully folding the photo and putting it back in my pocket. "We will find her," I insisted. "In fact . . .

"I think I know where Harper is."

13

JOE

"JOE, DEAR, DID YOU WANT ANOTHER doughnut?"

Harper's aunt Patty held out a near-empty box from her perch on the end of the bench.

"Uh, no thanks," I said, adjusting my binoculars.

"How about you, Officer McGill?" Patty asked.

"No thanks," he said. "I'm good with coffee."

The three of us were packed—along with Frank, Jones, and Officer Gomez—onto a wooden bench on the Atlantic City boardwalk. It was cold, being only a few minutes before ten on a March morning, but at least we had hot coffee and doughnuts that Frank, Jones, and I had picked up on the drive from Bayport.

"Won't you give me a hint?" Officer Gomez asked us. "I've always been the nice one to you boys, remember."

I raised an eyebrow at her. "I'm not so sure about that."

She frowned. "Well, I am genuinely nicer. Usually." She gave me an appealing look. "Come on, tell me what we're doing here."

Frank cleared his throat from Gomez's other side. "That will all be clear very soon," he said.

McGill looked up and down the line of us on the bench. "Obviously we're all people connected to Harper and her case," he said impatiently.

"Yup," said Frank, taking a sip of his coffee.

McGill fiddled with the lid on his own coffee, getting more and more frustrated. "You're seriously not going to tell us?!"

Frank glanced at me and shook his head. "You'll find out soon enough."

Officer McGill was pretty annoyed Frank wasn't telling them what he'd figured out. Now he sipped his coffee and narrowed his eyes. "I don't like games. And I don't have all morning."

It was definitely risky not to inform the police of our theory, and the officers certainly could have made us tell them our plans. But it seemed we had earned their respect on this case. Or they were worried about what we'd say about our interrogation—it's not usually a good idea to question minors without a guardian present. Whatever the reason, they were following our lead. Not that they were happy about it.

"Don't worry. You won't have to wait much longer," I assured them.

We looked around the boardwalk, from the just-opened arcade plus gift shop, to a saltwater taffy shop (a different one from Fiorelli's, and I made a mental note to check it out later), to a line of cheesy "boardwalk games," where you could win a huge stuffed animal. Farther down the boardwalk, the casinos were lined up, one after another, and an amusement park, still closed for the season, jutted out into a pier.

There weren't many boardwalk revelers around at this hour. Just a few joggers and a couple of people with metal detectors, wandering the beach.

Officer Gomez pointed to the white building that rose above the arcade/gift shop. "You guys keep looking up at this place," he said. "Is that something?"

I followed his eyes up the side of the white-painted building. A few small balconies jutted out from the wall. At the very top, an old-fashioned metal sign proclaimed the building THE SANDPIPER APARTMENTS.

"It most certainly is something," I replied.

Frank pulled out his phone and checked it, prompting me to look at mine. It was exactly 9:59. He and I nodded at each other.

"Ladies and gentlemen," said Frank, "I'd like to direct everyone's attention to a trash can across the boardwalk."

Everyone looked. "Which one?" Officer McGill demanded.

I pointed. "The one in front of the saltwater taffy shop just to the left of the Sandpiper apartment complex."

Everyone turned to face that garbage can. At the moment, absolutely nothing was happening.

McGill groaned. "Are you *serious!*—"

"Shhhhh," I hissed.

Because right at that moment, a hunched, slight figure was pushing open the front door of the Sandpiper. A baseball cap was pulled low over their head, and a baggy hoodie and sweats covered most of their body. The figure walked outside and slowly moved over to the trash can we were all watching, looked around furtively, and glanced pointedly at a corner of the arcade. Then, carefully, with shaking hands, the figure placed a wrapped plastic parcel in the trash can.

Frank cleared his throat and stood up, putting his coffee down on the bench behind him. "Hey," he yelled, "*Harper!*"

The figure looked up, seeking him out.

I gasped.

Even though her hair was shorter and dyed black, and she wasn't wearing any makeup, I would have recognized her anywhere. "Harper!"

Frank had explained his theory to Jones and me over and over the night before. Jones had even found some really useful information online to back it all up. But it was still a shock to see Harper alive and well, just with a different look.

Jones jumped to her feet and ran toward the hooded figure. "Oh my God, Harper!" she cried, her voice tight with worry.

Frank and I quickly followed behind her.

Just then another figure emerged from the Sandpiper. It was Complainy Guy, just as we'd hoped. Eyebrows furrowed, he reached into the pocket of his denim jacket and brandished a tiny gun in Frank's direction. . . .

But he quickly paled when he saw Detectives Gomez and McGill followed us from the bench. McGill pulled out his badge as he approached.

"Drop it," Gomez barked.

Complainy Guy dropped his gun onto the boardwalk and put his hands up.

"And if you point out your accomplice before we find her," Frank told him, "I bet that'll look good for you."

Complainy Guy scowled but pointed with one raised hand to the far wall of the Sandpiper, where a small alley led to a ramp off the boardwalk. . . .

"Come out, Geraldine. Trust me, it's better to cooperate," he yelled out. *This must not be the first time he's gotten into trouble with the police.*

Geraldine, the UrMotel host, reluctantly emerged with her hands up. "And just what are we being arrested for?" she sneered. Officer Gomez moved behind her and ushered her closer to Officer McGill.

To everyone's surprise, it was Harper who spoke up. "For

helping me stage my own abduction and run away from all my debts." She sighed and looked over to Patty. "I'm so sorry, Auntie."

"Oh, honey," Patty murmured, staring at Harper, who was looking down the line of us, biting her lip. "I'm just so relieved you're really okay! How—" She turned around and sought out Frank. "How did you figure this out?"

"Well . . . ," Frank began.

It was the gun that had tipped him off. Specifically, the way Von described the gun Complainy Guy had used to threaten him. *Super tiny*, he'd said.

That had reminded Frank of another time he and I had been threatened with a gun. It hadn't been that long ago.

Geraldine, the UrMotel host, had pointed a gun at us when she'd found us with Matt in Harper's room. Like the one Complainy Guy had threatened Von with, it was small. *Notably* small.

Which made Frank wonder: Could her gun be the same gun as Complainy Guy's?

And if it was—if they were working together—what exactly were they trying to *do*?

That's when Frank had started thinking about Harper. All the debts she'd racked up, and her tempestuous relationship with Matt, who seemed to want more from her than she could give. To put it plainly, Harper had a lot to gain from disappearing. If "Harper" was gone, then the Girl Formerly Known as Harper would get to keep all the money she stole, avoid her online victims and collections agents, and get out of her relationship with Matt, which clearly wasn't normal or healthy. Maybe she could even use that money—some of it, anyway—to start a new life in a city, going to art school, like she'd always wanted.

"But not all the money," Frank explained now. Some of it, he went on, she used to buy Geraldine's "help" to disappear. Because *that* was Geraldine's real business—not the UrMotels, though those were a profitable side gig. Geraldine worked with Complainy Guy to stage "abductions" for guests who wanted a fresh start. No one would ever know what happened to them. She'd done it before, with the other guests Gomez and McGill had mentioned who had "disappeared" from UrMotels in the area. And she'd tried to do it for Harper.

Complainy Guy ran interference at the UrMotel— kicking out any stray guests and creating believable suspects like the ones Harper cooperatively brought into the apartment. He'd encouraged her to bring back friends she made at Comic-Con. And he got rid of Von because he came too late, and they couldn't have anything disrupting Harper's "abduction." Because Geraldine owned the unit, she knew exactly where to place a plant to block the security camera.

As Frank explained, everyone stared at him, looking stunned. Even Complainy Guy and Geraldine looked shocked that we'd been able to figure it all out.

"But how did you find out for sure?" Gomez asked, gesturing at Harper. "How did you get her out here?"

Frank smiled at me. "That was Joe's idea."

Everyone turned to face me, and I felt a little self-conscious. "We slipped a note under the door of apartment 2G, the place where Complainy Guy was staying the night we met him. The police had called him a neighbor, so we figured he was a more permanent resident than he had claimed," I explained. "We'd already guessed that he worked for Geraldine and was in on the whole fake abduction. He's too big to be one of the actual abductors, so I'm guessing there two more people involved. Anyway, in the note we pretended to be one of the guys Harper owed money to, and we said we'd figured out the whole disappearance act and would tell everyone the truth—unless Harper herself came out and returned our money. We even asked they meet us here, at the Sandpiper, so they would know how much we'd figured out. That's what she was dropping in the trash can." I looked at Geraldine. "We knew Geraldine and her muscle would be nearby, making sure it all went off without a hitch."

"That's pretty good detective work," McGill murmured. He sounded, annoyingly, kind of surprised. Then there was silence for a few seconds.

Finally Patty spoke. "So you were going to disappear forever?" she asked Harper, shaking her head. "You were going to leave and never come back?"

Harper began to cry. "Aunt Patty . . . I really am sorry. It just seemed . . ."

"Easier?" Jones asked. When Harper nodded, Jones said,

"According to my research, the other two people who 'disappeared' from Geraldine's units were never found. No charges were ever filed. But as Detectives Gomez and McGill told us, those people had reasons to want to disappear too. But they weren't just running from their past. They had done some pretty bad stuff and were running from the law. I just can't believe you'd want to work with these guys."

Officer Gomez looked at Geraldine. "Do you have anything to say about that?"

Geraldine was still standing with her hands up. This time her shirt had a rhinestoned pineapple on it. Her jaw was set, and she didn't look sorry. She just shook her head. Her orange-tinted hair didn't move.

Gomez sighed. "All right," she said. "We'll have plenty of time to discuss this back at the station."

McGill gestured to Complainy Guy to follow him to the unmarked police car they had parked close by. But as Gomez moved toward Geraldine, the old woman suddenly bolted down the boardwalk.

"HEY!" Gomez screamed.

"Hey!" yelled a popcorn seller whose stand Geraldine plowed into, knocking the whole thing over.

I turned to Frank. "Come on!"

McGill stayed behind with Complainy Guy, but Frank and I followed Officer Gomez as she trailed Geraldine into the arcade and paused at the entrance. The inside was dark and musty, and the loud bleeps and bloops from the machines were a little overwhelming. A guy stood at a glass display case of cheap prizes, but he goggled at Gomez, who gestured that he should get out of there. He ran out the front door without a word.

I drew up behind her. "Where did she go?"

Gomez startled and looked at me, surprised. "I'm not sure," she admitted. "It's so dark in here. I thought I saw her run off to the left when she came in, but I don't know. . . ."

"We'll split up," I said, as Frank skidded to a stop behind me. "You take the back, by the Skee-Ball; I'll take the right, the gift shop; Frank, you take the left, the arcade games."

Gomez nodded. "Deal," she said, heading to the back of the arcade.

As Frank headed toward the bleeping arcade games, I walked into the grimy, seen-better-days gift shop. It was full of shelves of dusty merchandise that had probably been there since the 1980s. I stumbled into a rack of T-shirts, which included one with Garfield saying THE ONLY THING I LOVE MORE THAN LASAGNA IS PLAYING THE SLOTS IN ATLANTIC CITY!

"Aaarrgh!" I heard Frank yell. "She popped up behind the Whac-A-Mole machine! Get her!"

As I moved toward the arcade section, I heard Gomez shout.

"Joe!" she yelled. "Look out! She's coming your way!"

I ducked behind a shelf full of shell ashtrays and waited. Sure enough, she ran into the store area and looked around, creeping behind the personalized mugs.

I jumped out. "AHA!"

She saw me. "You'll never get me alive!"

I was impressed: that was an awfully spunky thing for such an old lady to say. My grandma lived in a retirement home and spent her golden days playing bridge and watching game shows I didn't know they made anymore. Geraldine ran a crime ring.

I advanced on her. Despite her spunkiness, I was bigger and stronger. "That's where you're wrong."

CRASH!!! Something hit me in the side of the head and knocked me down, and I was stunned by the sounds of shells clacking together and breaking glass. I blinked, struggling to keep conscious, and stared as a large periwinkle shell painted with a neon ATLANTIC CITY 2019 swam in my vision.

She'd knocked over the tank full of hermit crabs! This woman was diabolical!

"Frank . . . ," I moaned.

And then he was looming over me. "Get up, dude! She threw that tank at you and took off out the front door!"

"But the craaaaaabs!" I whined, pointing at Mr. Atlantic City 2019, who clicked his front claws at me.

Frank gasped. "That's cold! We'll help them when we've caught her. Come on."

I staggered to my feet and shook my head to try to clear it. Unfortunately, that only made it hurt a lot worse. But I managed to follow Frank out of the arcade and onto the boardwalk, which seemed blindingly bright now.

I scanned the stands. "She's not at the goldfish throw. Not at the Super Shot."

Frank pointed. "There!"

She was running past the food stands across from the games.

"HEY!" I yelled, bolting after her. She opened the door of an enclosed lemonade stand.

Finally I was too quick for her. I reached the door and pushed it open before she could block it off with a case of lemons.

"Come on, Geraldine," I coaxed. "You're not making things any easier for yourself. Aren't you in enough trouble, without resisting arrest?"

She scowled. "What do you know about it?"

"I know what it's like to get in over my head," I said, thinking of the SATs. "I know what it's like to get absorbed in something I shouldn't and forget what's really important."

She stared at me, her gaze softening a bit. "You do, huh?"

I nodded. "But it's never too late, you know," I said. "You could start cooperating. I can go back and do my SAT practice tests."

"What?"

"Never mind." I shook my head, moving even closer. She was backed up against the rear wall of the stand, and I was just a couple of feet away. I just had to reach out and grab her, and this would be over. "The point is, we can both turn things around!"

"BANZAI!"

Whack!

Something hit me square in the cheekbone, and I shrieked, grabbing at my face.

Whack! Whack! Whack!

One caught me on the ear. One hit my chest. It was lemons! Geraldine was now throwing lemons at me from a basket full of them!

Squish!

And some of them were *rotten!*

Where is the stand employee for all this? Are they hiding in here?

But I didn't have time to give it too much thought. Geraldine had thrown me off my game enough to slip past me and run out of the stand. Frank raised his arms as I emerged, sticky with lemon juice. "Dude, who is this lady? She slipped by me too. I barely even saw her!"

I could only shrug in response.

Frank pointed behind him. "She's down at the next line of stores."

Without further ado, we ran after her.

Gomez was already there, standing in front of the first store, a closed ice cream shop.

"Do we know where she is?" Frank asked her, panting.

Gomez shook her head. "She's slippery," she said. "Amazingly so, for her age."

"Tell me about it," I muttered, rubbing my cheek. I

looked at the stores. Only two were open: a swimsuit shop, and yet another saltwater taffy place.

"I'll take the bathing suits," Frank said, nodding at me.

I took a deep breath. *Yes.* All was as it should be. "I'll take the taffy."

"Whoever finds her, flush her out, and I'll be waiting here," said Gomez.

I walked into the saltwater taffy shop.

Inside, there were a few tall displays of boxes of taffy in different designs. One Atlantic City theme, one general beach theme, one "thank you" theme . . . They were all arranged around a large machine in the middle that mixed and pulled the taffy. It was running, and full of thick, gooey, delicious-looking taffy.

There was also a small desk in the rear with a cash register on it. Behind it, in the corner, I saw a terrified sales clerk about my age. She stared at me, clearly wondering who I was and why I'd chased an orange-haired woman in a pineapple top into her store.

Clunk. A few boxes fell off a display toward the rear of the store, across from the cashier's desk.

I whirled around, and there she was.

Geraldine. She cackled at me.

"Let's end this, Geraldine," I said.

"Ha! You going to try to bond with me over your SATs again, *boy?*"

I lunged at her, knocking over several boxes of taffy in the process. She backed up against the wall, picked some boxes off the shelf there, and started throwing them at me. They fell open, and little individually wrapped candies flew everywhere. The cashier girl darted out from behind the desk and ran right out the front door. I didn't blame her.

I caught one of the boxes of taffy and winged it back at Geraldine. "ENOUGH! We're wasting taffy, and that's just wrong."

Geraldine cackled again, grabbing a ceramic sandcastle off the shelf. "You like taffy? Can't stand it myself. Too sticky!"

Now I was really mad. *The stickiness is the best part!*"

She chucked the sandcastle at me. I ducked. It hit the window behind me and shattered it with a crash.

Frank and Officer Gomez must have heard the noise, because soon they were running toward us and the three of us were able to corner Geraldine in the store. Finally she was trapped.

Back at the bench where everyone else had waited, Harper was speaking tearfully with her aunt Patty. When Patty saw Frank and me walking over, she waved us closer.

Patty was teary too, we could see now. "I'm trying to explain," she said, "why what Harper did upset me so much."

Harper wiped her eye with the back of her hand. "I never wanted to hurt you, Aunt Patty," she said. "I guess I just thought it would be *easier* for you. You gave up a lot to take care of me. I love you, but I wanted you to be free."

Patty stared at her. "Free?" she asked. "How could I ever be free, not knowing where you were, not knowing if you were even safe? I love you, girl. Don't you understand that?"

Harper's face crumpled into a sob. "I think I forget sometimes," she whimpered.

Frank cleared his throat. "Harper," he said, "it's fine for you to try to turn over a new leaf, and make yourself happy . . . but you can't con people out of their money, or lie to people who care about you. That's what made what Geraldine is doing wrong."

Harper sniffled. "I think I'm starting to get that," she said. "I just . . . I don't know. I was feeling so . . ."

". . . desperate?" I suggested.

She looked at me, her eyes lighting with surprise. "Yes," she said. "That's it. Desperate."

"Lot of that going around lately," Frank muttered.

I looked at Harper. "You should know," I said, "that Matt agrees your relationship should end. He knows he was too controlling and way out of line. He's going to work on it."

Harper looked briefly relieved, but then her gaze became dark again. "He'll have to work on it alone," she said.

I nodded. "He knows. And it's probably a good idea for you to stay away from each other. But you don't have to worry about him."

Harper looked relieved again. She took in a breath, then let it out slowly. She looked around at Patty, Jones, Frank, and me.

"I'm sorry, all of you," she said. "I'm so sorry I brought you all into this. Geraldine told me I needed a reason to stay at the UrMotel to give to my friends and family. Something plausible so they wouldn't be suspicious about me coming to this town. I was worried about running into some of the people I'd tricked on InkWorld, but I didn't want to miss the opportunity to meet you in person, Jones. It was such a fun day, and I thought of it as my last hurrah. But I see now how many problems I caused. I didn't think people would feel that way about me, and I'm sorry I freaked you out."

There were murmurs of appreciation from everyone, and Jones stepped forward. "I'm just glad you're okay," she said. "I know you're still working things out, but I hope we can keep in touch."

Harper looked at her, clearly touched. "Thanks, Jones."

I looked down the boardwalk. Officers Gomez and McGill were leading a handcuffed Geraldine back toward us. I could see Complainy Guy already sitting in the back of the police car.

"Harper," Gomez called to our teary friend. "You'll have to come down for questioning too. Can you follow us to the station?"

Harper nodded. "Of course."

"We should really thank you boys," Officer McGill told us. "I know I didn't trust you before, but you've been invaluable on this case. We never would have solved it without you."

I smiled. *Man, that never gets old.* "Well," I said happily, putting my arm around Frank's shoulders, "this is just one more successful case solved by the Hardy boys!"

Something shoved between us. Some*one*. "And Jones!"

Suddenly Jones was standing between Frank and me, an arm around each of our waists, smiling a blindingly white smile. I stared down at her.

"Sure," I muttered, wondering how long I'd have to put up with this. "And Jones."

But then I saw how Frank was beaming at her—and me. And I remembered how Jones had helped us figure out Harper's passwords and did tons of Internet research and kind of saved my life when Matt was after me with a hunting rifle.

Okay, so Jones wasn't a Hardy. So she got in the way of Frank and Joe time. So she could be annoying.

Still, I had to admit to myself—she wasn't *that* bad.

SECOND CHANCES

14

FRANK

A FEW WEEKS LATER I WAS READING in my room when Joe came barging in with his laptop.

"Okay, dude. Moment of truth and I need some support here."

"SAT results?" I asked as he plopped down on my bed.

"Yup." I watched his eyes scan the screen—and then saw his face fall.

"Ugh," he said.

"That bad?" I asked gently.

He shook his head, putting the computer down. "Let's just say . . . I didn't do very well."

I scratched my ear, suddenly feeling awkward. "I'm sorry, dude. We had a lot going on that week."

Joe shrugged. "It's not surprising, I guess. Still, I'm disappointed."

"Well . . . ," I said, trying to find the right words to comfort him. "We *did* find a missing girl and shut down a UrMotel-based crime ring!"

Joe nodded. "Right, that's something," he said, but his voice didn't sound completely sincere. "Speaking of which, did I tell you? I got an e-mail from Harper the other day. Her apartment is really small, but overall, she's having a really good time in the city. She's learning now to bartend and hopes to use her earnings to keep paying back all the money she owes. And once she's done with that: art school. She did get a ton of community service for all that fraud stuff, but it sounds like even that's going well." He smiled, and that, at least, seemed genuine.

"That's great," I said. "Good for her, landing on her feet. And I'm glad we managed to shut down Geraldine's business before someone got hurt."

Joe grunted. Geraldine hadn't exactly gone quietly—she'd been feisty in the preliminary hearings for the case against her—but the evidence against her was pretty damning. It looked like she had been behind the two other "disappearances" in the area, and those people had now been found and had to face all the things they'd been trying to escape. It was hard to believe Geraldine would escape conviction.

As I'd spoken, Joe had opened up his test scores again and was frowning at them.

"Hey," I said, putting my hand over the scores. "You know, the SATs happen again in a few months—and as long as no serious mysteries happen, I can help you study? It's not easy to be a teen detective and a scholar—but it *is* possible. I mean, just look at me." I grinned.

Joe rolled his eyes, but then nodded. "Okay. You're on." He saved a file of his test scores to his desktop, naming it *TO BE CONTINUED*. "We just have to hope nothing mysterious is happening in a few months. . . ."

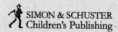

New mystery. New suspense. New danger.

Nancy Drew
DIARIES™

BY CAROLYN KEENE

NANCYDREW.COM

EBOOK EDITIONS ALSO AVAILABLE

From Aladdin | simonandschuster.com/kids